DAUGHTER
OF NIGHT

DAUGHTER OF NIGHT

A TALE OF THREE WORLDS

by Lydia Obukhova

TRANSLATED BY MIRRA GINSBURG

MACMILLAN PUBLISHING CO., INC.
New York

1 2 3 4 5 6 7 8 9 10

Library of Congress Cataloging in Publication Data
Obukhova, Lidiia Alekseevna.
Daughter of night; a tale of three worlds.
Translation of Lilit.
[1. Science fiction] I. Title.
PZ7.016Li3   [Fic]   74–6274   ISBN 0–02–768500–4

Ob

to B.G.

CONTENTS

Quotations at the beginning of chapters
are by the Russian Symbolist poet
Maximilian Voloshin (1877–1932).

"Lilith herself destroyed her house
and went away to unknown places
where no one had set foot before."
—*from a Sumerian myth*

TABUNDA

"And all that is
Began through rebellion."

T HE STAR traversed the circles of the Universe.

Unwatched by any eye on Earth, it stubbornly sent out the alphabet of its pulsing beam. But animals moved on a horizontal plane. And human beings did not see the night sky—it was obliterated by the feeble glow of their fires. They had no intimation of the vast and multiple dimensions of space.

The Star was approaching, but it was still very far, at a distance of several planetary generations. . . .

Lilith woke suddenly. It seemed to her that no more time had passed between falling asleep and waking than would be needed for a wave of the hand. But actually she had slept through two fires. The sun had long gone down, and the black sky was caught in a tangle of branches.

She was awakened by the sound of the drum. She raised her head. That day the tribe had been successful in its hunt. Only one hunter was injured: the claws of the dying beast had torn the skin on his shoulder. But the blood was quickly stopped, and now he was celebrating with the others by the common fire.

Lilith stretched her neck with curiosity. Like all the children of the tribe, she slept behind a palisade which was too high for any animal to leap over. The bedding of freshly gathered grass sent up a dense fragrance, covering all other smells. Before turning into a pile of yellow husks, the wilting greenery exhaled moisture. The leaves were still alive, and the flowers lay with open mouths like fish cast out on the shore; for the first time their crowns had not closed at nightfall.

Lilith tried to drive away the clinging smell. Her eyes greedily sought to catch glints from the fire. The smoky, reddish dusk rang with the sounds of the tabunda—each stroke distinct and separate like the sudden throbbing of blood in the body. They passed through Lilith's veins like jets of flame, now chilling, now burning her.

Troubled, she nudged one sleeper, another, a third. She nudged them roughly, as a creature accustomed to feeling pain and to inflicting it on others without giving it much thought. Pain wasn't like hunger—it did not matter.

But no one woke. For the others, the day was quite enough; they fell asleep before sundown. For them, the sun never stopped its procession. And if they were roused by their elders over some nocturnal alarm, they merely blinked in confusion, the alarm seeming a part of their dreams.

But Lilith had known from childhood about the existence of night—the other side of the world. She had been told about it by her mother, who had given birth to her near midnight. Her very name, Lilith, meant darkness, the deepest darkness when even the infrequent stars were hidden behind clouds. And everyone wondered: why had such a frightening name been chosen for her? All the other women placed their children under the protection of daytime powers. But Lilith's mother wanted her daughter to be the daughter of the night. Perhaps the ailing woman had hoped that her child would be the one to overstep the terrors of the night, as the brave step over a magic circle.

Her mother had never spoken to Lilith about this. They saw each other seldom. Weaned children were brought up by the old women of the tribe, while the younger women and the men were busy securing food.

The people of Tabunda, "they who created the drum," had long walked through the forest, stopping only to hunt. They strove with all their energy to find an open space, a grassy plain like the one they had come from. They felt buried in the forest. Its hostile watchfulness oppressed them. There were no paths in it except the paths of animals. Occasional encounters with other humans left them baffled: the men of the woods were wild and timid; they saw an enemy in every corner and vanished before they could be hailed. And the tribe walked and walked among the giant trees, which exuded translucent amber resin. Lilith did not know when the great exodus had begun and what had caused it. She was born on the way. To her the forest was home, and the fallen trunks, chewed up by rodents, a cradle and a refuge. But Lilith's mother used to say that she remembered a night sky with many fires. Until the end, until her early death (she had been bitten by a snake), Lilith's mother had languished under the low ceiling of the trees, through which only an occasional star managed to send a distorted, elongated image of brightness.

But it is doubtful that even her mother had seen that endless sky—she had been so young, and the forest was so vast! In her simplicity, her inability to distinguish between her own self and others, she may have populated her memory with tales she had heard from older people. The tribe had no way of measuring time; life on the plain seemed only yesterday.

Where were the people of Tabunda going? Where did all human tribes flow in their wanderings? Like water, they were filling all the hollows of the planet.

Somewhere in the north grazed musk-oxen. In the thickets there were forest elephants. Spotted horses, large-headed, with big teeth and narrow muzzles, neighed fiercely, galloping over the plains. But all that was a vanishing world.

The earth had taken three deep breaths, now closing the frozen eyes of continents, now opening them wide. When they were opened, the lakes left by the melting glaciers looked trustingly into the sky. Then everything froze again, cold winds dried out the land; it cracked, and yellowish dust was carried over thousands of miles until it settled somewhere in a layer of fertile loam. And after all this, man appeared—first in the gloomy forests, and later on the green plains.

drum rang and rang. Its broken rhythms drew her forcefully. They seemed to pulse within her, like the first call of awakening life.

Lilith shook the stakes that formed the palisade till they were loose. Then she spread them apart and thrust her head out, then her narrow shoulders. Ignoring scratches, she broke out like an animal escaping from a snare.

Her eyes soon grew accustomed to the dark. She noticed with astonishment that she distinguished everything around her almost as clearly as in the day-time.

The boundless forest seethed with nocturnal passions, with the chase of the strong after the weak. The flame of the bonfire looked like an open wound.

The coldness of the dew recalled her to herself. The fire was nearer now, the fence was left behind. It seemed to her that many eyes were staring at her: the eyes of the trees, of the grass, of the flames. . . . She held her breath. In just a moment the punishing claws of some beast would strike her down from behind. The girl waited for retribution. Shivers ran down her skin as if she were a frightened wolf cub.

Yet Lilith did what countless people had done before her and would do after her: she did not allow fear to master her. The instinct of self-preservation serves alike to breed cowards and prompt courage. For there are two ways of escaping danger—by running from it or by meeting it and learning its reality.

He was small and insignificant, but he wa
helpless.

The history of the Tabunda tribe began wi
creation of the drum. The skin of an animal ki
the men was drawn over a circle woven of
twigs. When the last drops of moisture in th
dried out, the drum became light and taut. Th
est touch made it quiver and emit strange
still infinitely far from music, but already
and exciting.

The tabunda, the drum, belonged to r
was brought from place to place with grea
tected against harm and rain. It was
everyone's. Even the tiniest infants were
times to bring down their swarthy, grimy
upon its singing skin.

The tribe began to call itself Tabunda
of the sound of the drum. When, on a v
night after a successful hunt, the peo
reluctant to go to sleep, would draw
heat of the fire and form a circle, th
come into its own. Each man wante
courage, to embellish his exploits. A
were still few, he whirled and leaped
and, of course, he beat the drum:
the greater seemed the drummer's pr

When she was first awakened
the tabunda, Lilith had no though
taboo; with the coming of twili
not to leave the fenced-in sleep

Lilith crept forward.

And the tabunda boomed and boomed, and the fragrance of the roasted meat on which the adults had feasted after the lucky hunt hung peacefully over the clearing.

When Lilith reached the age preceding adulthood, a web of taboos was imposed upon her, restricting her at every step. Now she no longer slept with the children behind the fence. But there was an invisible circle around the camp site that she was not allowed to cross. This circle, however, widened after every march.

The people of Tabunda had been walking so long that their skin had turned pale from the damp perpetual twilight of the forest. But they had learned a great deal. They learned from their earliest years to recognize the tracks of wild boar and forest antelopes. They distinguished unerringly between trees with soft wood and those with wood hard enough for making darts. They were skilled at gathering young shoots, catching edible insects, and finding birds' eggs. They lived like all men in those distant times, searching for food and walking indifferently past iron ores.

One day in early summer the women of the tribe set out for a distant marsh along the river. They would be gone for many days, digging with twigs and hands through fields of sticky mud overgrown with reeds, searching for edible bulbs and tubers. During their absence, the younger children were left in the care of the adolescents. Lilith, the eldest, went out daily at dawn to wander about in the vicinity of the camp. She returned at noon, her woven basket almost always filled with bright-skinned little fruits. The fruits were wrapped in bark and baked in hot coals. She also brought dark fibrous roots which were roasted and given to the children, who chewed them thoroughly, extracting the gummy sap. Sometimes she was lucky and killed a lizard or found large white caterpillars. They had to be content with any food they could obtain until the women returned with the tubers and baked flatcakes, or the men came with some forest animal brought down by their darts.

Although the woods were pierced with threads of sunlight in the daytime, Lilith did not venture too far into their depths. She knew that the forest, like the water, was ready to swallow the careless without mercy. Man had not yet become the master of dry land, just as today he is not master of the seas and oceans; even in an ordinary stagnant pool, life still proceeds according to its own laws.

Lilith walked, stepping flatly on her whole foot, and yet her steps seemed soundless, as though the feet had an intelligence of their own and chose their own path while she looked warily around for hidden dangers.

Suddenly the shadow of a man fell on the ground before her. In an instant her glance slid from the long legs and narrow hips to the high chest and muscular neck bearing a head with ears set close to the skull, which lent the face an aspect both brutish and at the same time nobly human. Faded, reddish-brown strands of hair, encircled with a strip of bark, fell on the man's forehead.

The shadow still lay on Lilith's bare feet, but the tension had already left her body. She took a deep breath of relief. The man was Odam. They had grown up together, and it was only in the past year that they had been separated. Odam had been initiated into the society of hunters, while Lilith still remained under the supervision of the mothers.

For a few moments they faced each other shyly. On top of the food in Lilith's basket lay two round shiny fruits. They were still unripe, and their thin layer of pulp would prickle the tongue; nevertheless, they could be eaten. Lilith had managed to knock them down from the topmost branches of the tree. A small patch of sunlight fell on the fruits through the dense foliage above, and their shiny skins glowed like tongues of flame.

"Give me," said Odam. Then he smiled and said, "Your face is pleasing and fair." This was the usual formula of polite greeting. After a moment he added, "You are grown up now."

He stretched his hand to the basket. Lilith drew back, offended. Had he forgotten that girls of her age were not permitted to speak with men?

Odam continued to regard her with a smile, but

she sprang aside, like a young tree straightening up, and walked away. She put her basket on her head, and from behind she looked like a jar with two bent handles.

"Heo!" he called out after her in a puzzled voice. Then he repeated impatiently, "Heo?"

Then Lilith cried out without turning, "I have not passed the initiation rites, don't you remember? We may not speak!"

There was a troubled silence behind her. Odam himself had only recently become an adult hunter. The customs of the tribe were sacred to him, yet now he had broken one! This threw him into confusion. But still he followed the girl, with his head bent low.

"We can walk together without speaking," he muttered, looking aside.

She did not open her lips. Her eyes, always elusive and a little wild, now stubbornly looked straight ahead. Odam walked half a step behind her, as was proper for a man, in order to protect the woman from unexpected danger.

The forest opened before them and closed as they passed. Lianas and vines formed patterned walls between the trunks. Sparks of sunlight danced on the green moss. Every fallen tree gave refuge to countless tribes of insects. Flashing their metallic backs, they scuttled over the dead bark; they flew about, chattering and buzzing in their insatiable hunger to live out their short lives as quickly as possible. Pale clusters of rapacious flowers opened their sticky mouths. In the upper levels of the green ceiling birds called to one another: Gorral-kor! Varr! Week-week!

Their voices were so loud that for a moment the girl and the young man stopped and threw their heads back, peering up with childlike curiosity. The birds continued their frenzied clicks and calls. Odam clicked his tongue, imitating the sound. Lilith threw him a sidelong, approving glance.

"Take," said Odam suddenly, as he caught her glance. He pulled the bundle of small game from behind his shoulder and held it out to the girl.

"Your hand is generous and kind," she whispered, dropping her eyes.

Their young bodies were suddenly seized with such hunger that they halted at once and squatted down to make a fire. Odam rolled a stick between his palms, pressing its sharpened end into a hollow in a piece of soft wood, while Lilith carefully filled the hollow with a tuft of dry moss resembling pale green fur.

Waiting until the flames burned down and they could roast the skinned animal on the glowing coals, Odam and Lilith sat facing each other across the fire. They did their best to preserve the remnants of silence.

To keep her hair from being singed, Lilith tied it back with a string of grass which she quickly braided as she sat. Like all the members of the tribe, she had slender pliant fingers, able to perform any needed task.

A tasty smell rose from the meat, roasting in its cradle of sand.

Odam curbed his impatience. He did not want to do what some of the other men did when hungry—cut a slice of raw meat just barely touched by the fire, and eat it. He wanted to wait and to receive his food from Lilith's hands.

He suddenly recalled a day when they were still small children. They had been gathering snails by a forest lake, and when they broke the first shell, the bitter liquid burned their mouths. The snail they tasted was not edible.

He laughed gaily at the memory but immediately clicked his tongue, annoyed with himself. Lilith might think he was laughing at her. He tried to explain it to her and passed his index finger down from his mouth, which meant poison. Lilith glanced back quickly, thinking that he was warning her of a snake. Odam shook his head reassuringly.

"Bitter snail," he said, unable to continue silent. "Remember? A long time ago, by the lake. We were like fawns."

They laughed in relief, looking at each other across the wavering hot air over the fire. The common memory restored Lilith's trust.

"Are the men returning? Was the hunt successful?" the girl now asked, settling down more comfortably and putting her chin on her bent knee.

"The men are returning," answered Odam. "But they are still far. The hunt was successful."

"Your feet are light and fast," said Lilith approvingly, with another sidelong glance.

After eating, they quenched their thirst with the muddy water from the brook. The bronze sun had passed from their right to their left.

As they approached the camp, they slowed their steps. No one was to see them together.

Odam came up to Lilith and with a light movement passed his hand over her face and shoulders. That was how good dancers were thanked at celebrations. He did not know himself what he was thanking her for.

Lilith's skin was cool and smooth like a young frog's. Her quick evasive eyes, her pouting lips, her fast breath, her slender arms, thinner at the shoulder than at the elbow—all of this suddenly moved in upon him like a raincloud. The trembling of the earth passed into his knees. The moment was like the flash of burning heavenly root during a storm—both long and short. It jumbled time.

When they recalled themselves, the basket and the scattered fruit lay on one side, Odam's darts on the other. But for a long time they could not break their embrace. And it was only much later that they returned separately to the camp.

No one had noticed their long absence. The tribe hummed with excitement: their forest captivity was about to end! Three of the hunters had gone so far in their chase of an animal that they had caught sight of open space between the trees.

At first none of them understood the full meaning of what was gradually being revealed to their eyes. They merely noticed that the land was becoming dryer; instead of the solid wall of giant trees with dense, impenetrable crowns, they came upon wider and wider clearings; the tree trunks and the ground were no longer covered with thick, deadly pale moss with quivering, never-drying drops of dew on it; the pebbly, sandy soil absorbed the excess of moisture.

The going became easier and easier. New odors seeped into the air; the fetid dampness of swampy hollows overgrown with yellow water lilies had disappeared. The trackless, ancient forest through which several generations of Tabunda people had wandered was thinning out; the trees spread wider apart.

The hunters stopped, wary and confused. Their quarry escaped. They remembered it much later. Now there were no more trees before them, only a low wall of shrubs. Although the sun had not yet risen, some hooved animal grazed peacefully, crunching the leaves and juicy twigs. The wind blew in the direction of the hunters, and the animal was unaware of their presence.

Then one of the men took a step forward. The animal snorted and sprang aside. The Tabunda man

—the one who had taken the first step—stubbornly knit his eyebrows, as sharp and narrow as the blades of a stone knife, and rushed out recklessly. A moment, and he disappeared behind the shrubs.

The other two did not follow. Now and then they caught a glimpse of the one who had gone forward. He seemed tall, though he was merely lean, like all the men of the tribe. His face was framed in a sparse beard that concealed his chin and the thinness of his cheeks. A pebble in the shape of a fish with a hole worn in it by running water lay just beneath the hollow of his neck, suspended from a thick, dry tendon. Now the hollow was pulsing madly. He knew already that the tribe would name him "He Who Had First Come Out of the Forest"!

An altogether different terrain began after the shrubs. The ground was level, undulating slightly all the way to the chain of hills dissolving in the distance. Swirls of morning mist were rolling across the land, as if the earth itself were breathing and alive. The clusters of trees here and there rang with the chorus of bird song.

"Loo! Loo!" the hunter called to the others.

A cry of joy, the first human word flew over the happy plain. As the two who had hesitated came forward, tall grass sprang up before them suddenly like spray. Its stems gleamed with large drops of dew in the newly risen sun—a fiery disk they had never seen before. Something astonishing in its colors, smells,

and airy space was revealing itself to the men, intoxicating and overwhelming them. All three were
young hunters; neither they nor their elders had
ever known open grassland, and they stood transfixed
by the sight.

The men of Tabunda remained in the valley until
noon, and when the air cleared, they saw a mountain
range far in the distance, crowned by an immense,
dazzling-white summit that seemed to float in the
sky. They did not know as yet what it was, but it
awed them.

When the women who had gone out to the swamp
to gather bulbs had heard the news, they hastened to
the camp, still empty-handed, but no one reproached
them for it.

The tribe began to prepare for the long march,
anxious for the new sun to find them already on the
way. The protective fires burned almost until
dawn, and the men on guard struck the tabunda
from time to time, as though to drive away the evil
powers that might gather over the encampment.
Man's awareness, however, was not overburdened by
imagination. The people of Tabunda had the directness and the courage of indomitable health. The
riddles of the world still troubled them so little that
they passed through them as through light morning
mist which does not interfere with vision. Their eyes
were clear and turned only to the nearest objects.

And yet it took some time before they reached the

promised edge of the forest. It was as if the forest refused to let them go: tempests raged every night; lightning flared; now one and now another dried-out tree fell crashing to the ground with outspread branches, like a dying hunter. For trees, like people, died of wounds and of diseases.

The tribe moved slowly, but the more daring of the men went out more and more often to hunt on the plain, and brought back unfamiliar animals. They would return later than the others, tired but exultant. Jubilation infused the heartbeats of those who had been out in open space, as if their mighty chests had also turned into singing, humming tabundas.

Odam first saw the grassland in a silky, warm rain. For a long time he breathed in its fresh, clean wind, the smell of hills and bright green meadows. It seemed strange to be exposed and visible from every side; involuntarily he backed away toward the trees. But the illimitable light of day, which could not be compared to anything he knew, already took possession of him, and he stood with parted lips to breathe the light as though it were air.

These moments of release and freedom made clearer to him something within himself, for since the day when he had touched Lilith his life had been troubled and confused. He became sullen and awkward. Going out with the other hunters, he stumbled constantly; dry twigs kept snapping loudly under his feet. Bending over a forest stream, he delayed quenching his thirst, for everywhere he saw Lilith's quick eyes. His former sound sleep gave way to broken, brief periods of forgetfulness, from which he wakened several times at night. And it was only by extreme effort that he restrained himself from jumping up, from blindly thrusting aside his sleeping comrades and rushing out in search of the girl.

The fever of desire made him abandon all remnants of prudence, although this did not happen all at once.

One day Lilith passed by him at a distance of no more than three steps without noticing him. Her glance was tense, turned inward. And her hands, which appeared just as unseeing, carelessly squeezed the hollow shell of a large nut she carried. Silvery drops fell from the vessel, filled to the brim. They glinted in the sun and buzzed like a swarm of bees. This buzzing was, of course, heard only by Odam. He stood motionless while Lilith was walking by, and his lips felt scorched as though brushed by a dry burning twig. But when she disappeared, he fell with a moan to the ground where some drops had fallen, trying to cool his cheeks with that illusive moisture. Strange, confused feelings troubled him.

And it was only there, out on the open plain, that he suddenly knew what it was that he wanted: he wanted Lilith! Only Lilith! He wanted her to tend his fire and gather roots for him while he was hunting with the men. The sweet moment of returning to her arose before him with such vividness, as if they had lived together, in bodily union, for many years; as if they had lit fires together, scraped fresh skins, and later slept upon them feeling with their sides the pleasant warmth of the fur and of the glowing embers.

Among the people of Tabunda there was no compulsion in the choice of mates, but neither were they entirely free. There were complicated considerations of blood ties. And the opinion of kinsfolk who met in council to discuss the age, the health, the personal merits and abilities of the bride and groom was also important. Among these hidden obstacles, well-known to the adults but still unknown to Odam, he now had to set out on the journey toward his goal—receiving Lilith from the hands of the elders and giving himself to her, with all the rituals attending a marriage celebration.

True, before Lilith could be wooed, she still had to undergo the rites of initiation into adulthood, which consisted from time immemorial of the defloration of the girl by the lucky man of the tribe who managed to reach her first through the protective guard of women.

This was a gay, playful, sportive ceremony, in which the participants competed not only in agility and cunning but also in witticisms, in singing and dancing skill, in exchanging apt nicknames, and creating general merriment. The passive role was assigned to a single person—the girl herself, who, before becoming a woman with full rights and full participation in deciding tribal affairs, had to spend her final hours of childhood in absolute obedience. Her voice was not heard in the general hubbub. She sat in the half-dark hut awaiting him who would enter it.

A merry free-for-all, which sometimes turned into violence, would take place at the entrance to the hut, but all this reached the girl within as the noise of the waves might reach the bottom of a lake.

She took part in nothing and chose no one. And the man who first possessed her received no special rights to her. Even if the nocturnal mystery resulted in a child, it would be regarded as the child of the young woman's subsequent husband, not of the winner in the competition.

Odam felt no enmity toward his future brief rival. But could he await the ritual with equanimity now that he and Lilith had violated the taboo and carried a secret guilt before the tribe? He dreaded the heavy punishment that would be visited upon Lilith in accordance with established custom. There was only one way out: he, and only he, must win the competition and be the first to enter the hut. Just as, after that, only he must become Lilith's husband.

Odam returned from the plain with a fine quarry. Although the goat's sharp horns had torn one of his muscles, the wound was dressed with ash, and now

Odam, somewhat weakened from the loss of blood, was nevertheless in a heightened, almost intoxicated mood. It was the first time that he returned to the encampment not as one of the hunters but as a leader surrounded by the rest. He immediately went to search out his mother. Not because he felt particularly close to her but because she was one of the group of older women who watched over the purity of blood ties in the tribe and knew all the complicated bonds of kinship.

His mother sat on a sandy mound, weaving strips of willow bark into double ropes for fishing nets. This was the women's usual occupation during their free hours. The tribe needed many nets, for they broke easily: sharp underwater roots or large fish frequently tore holes in them.

On seeing Odam, his mother did not halt her work but merely compressed her lips, already slightly sunken, waiting to hear what he had to say. With the years, her face had become gaunt, and her eyebrows, meeting over her nose, lent her a somber, at times almost a fierce expression.

Odam placed a piece of liver, the reward of a successful hunter, on the mound before her. His mother accepted the gift politely. She was not surprised to learn that her grown son was thinking of marriage. She began to name all the suitable girls. Lilith's name was not among them. At first Odam thought the omission was due to the girl's age and he interrupted his mother anxiously: he was not seeking, he said, to become anyone's husband immediately; he was ready to wait for some others to grow up. He named several girls of Lilith's age. And again her name, which scalded his mouth and stopped his blood, passed unnoticed by his mother. In careful detail she continued to discuss the qualities of other girls. Odam fidgeted impatiently. Then came a blow, the full finality of which he did not even realize at once: his marriage to Lilith was impossible! They belonged to the same branch of kinship.

He listened to his mother a while longer, then stood up and walked away, carrying her piercing glance like an intolerable burden on his back.

To give up a woman when in his thoughts he had already lived a happy lifetime at her side? When every dream of his concluded with the moment of their union? Has this ever been possible to any man, before or after Odam?

For several days he went about in gloomy silence. He was in a state that either resolves itself in action or destroys the will. Odam's compliant, unrebellious nature might have led him to submit, were it not for Lilith herself.

She was passionately avid for the future. She was drawn to Odam as if he were a magnet: his touch remained in her memory like the fiery sting of a wasp. All the fear, and the release from fear, that had shaken her so violently as she was breaking the taboo had led her to associate that surge of inner strength with Odam. It seemed to her that only by cleaving to him would she at last find blessed relief from the new feelings that tormented her.

Lilith had changed not only inwardly but also in appearance, and this was noticed by everyone. The black hair, which she no longer covered with clay and grease, now floated in the air like a bird's wing, and wherever she passed, all eyes were on her with a vague, strange feeling, as though she might indeed soar up into the air at any moment and fly far, far away.

The beauty of Lilith, still an adolescent, drew many of the men. They followed her with their eyes. She troubled their sleep. The elders were already exchanging meaningful glances behind her back. And finally Lilith's initiation rites were set for the third day after the emergence from the forest.

Lilith sat in the semidarkness of the hut with a beating heart, trying to discover through the cracks who was succeeding in the competition. But the women surrounded her with a dense ring, and it was only from time to time that they cried out the names of the attackers.

Most prominent among the contenders was He Who Had First Come Out of the Forest. He had not been mistaken—this was his name now. But how he had changed since then! His glance was as cold as a black stone unwarmed by the sun. He was older and stronger than Odam, and his perseverance in seeking to break through to the hut compelled Odam to strain all his cunning.

The women, who had laughed at first as they repelled the many seekers, now fell involuntarily under the spell of the two leaders. Strong hands struck out hard, inflicting more and more fresh bruises. The first drops of blood appeared.

From what dark depths of time could it have come —this custom of defending the woman from the man? For even the great-great-grandmothers of Tabunda had not been threatened by anyone; they had full equality with the men—an equality necessitated by the hard, demanding life of the tribe.

For many years no girl had attracted as much attention as Lilith. Was she a beauty? But the concept of beauty changes with time. The men of Tabunda, wishing to praise a woman, would say: "Thy shoulders are wide, thy breast is full."

The elders of the tribe watched the heated struggle with some anxiety: the contenders might suffer serious injury. True, this was the first holiday since the people had come out of the forest. Before them spread the plain and the low chain of hills from which it was always easy to see the surrounding land and find the needed quarry to feed the tribe. They set up camp at the edge of the wood; they breathed the healthy air of the foothills, and the swampy lakes in the nearby forest supplied them with an abundance of tubers. The roots of unfamiliar grasses of the plain were still used with great caution.

How, then, could they refrain from celebrating the long-awaited exodus from the forest, along with the coming of age of a girl like Lilith? And the elders did not interfere in the contest; they shook their heads approvingly, proud of the women of Tabunda, who could be obtained only by dint of so much effort.

According to the terms of the game, the men were not to strike back; they were to break through only by the sheer weight of their bodies.

The women noticed the persistence of He Who Had First Come Out of the Forest, and they formed an even denser wall against him. His own wife, with cries of alternating jealousy and pity, struck him again and again. She vaguely remembered that he had not fought for her with such fierceness. Nevertheless, she was excited and gay like the rest: an ancient ritual was in progress—a new woman was entering the ranks of the tribe.

Odam was shunted out of the center of the struggle. His rival threw himself unflinchingly again and again, like a battering ram, against the wall of blows, breaking the ranks of the defenders of the hut. The other contenders had already stepped back, watching the battle. Odam's arms dropped with fatigue. But he stood motionless just long enough for the women to cease giving him any attention, and then with a desperate leap he flung himself under the feet of those who were at the end of the row, bruising his chest and face against the roots on the ground.

There was an outcry of dismay and resentment. He could still have been dragged away from the opening in the hut, but the elders saw Lilith stretch out her hand, and they struck the drum, announcing the end of the rite.

And yet the rival had been only half a step from Lilith! He threw at Odam a dark, cold glance, full of rage, but turned away at once with a feigned laugh. His wife put a hand on his bleeding shoulder. Together they walked away. Soon the voices of the others receded too. The sun set, festive fires were lit, a generous feast was to follow. No one thought of Odam and Lilith anymore.

For a time there was no sound but the young man's heavy, broken breathing; he saw something dark in the corner. It was Lilith. But she made no move toward him.

"Speak," whispered Odam, licking his cut lips. "When I hear your voice from afar, it is fragrant, like a branch in bloom. If you turn it to me, it will be filled with the juice of fruits."

He spoke as he did because his throat was parched. Odam's speech was simple and concrete, as was his thought.

Lilith understood and silently held out to him a hollowed vessel. Odam drank long and greedily. His eyes became accustomed to the dark: now he could distinguish the vague blur of Lilith's face and her black hair—blacker than the night itself. When he had quenched his thirst, the bitter thought stirred in him again: that night would be the only one in their whole lives! The morning would separate them forever. To Odam love meant only one thing: he hurried to receive what he desired. He stretched his arms toward the girl, seeking to draw her to himself. But she evaded him.

"I have only one heart," she said in a flat voice. "Let there not be two in you either."

This meant: don't lie, don't conceal, don't pretend.

"You know?" Odam muttered, discouraged.

"Yes," Lilith replied.

And suddenly she broke into sobs. Not as children whimper, but with the rage heard in a wild beast's cry. The fleeting joy of the impending night immediately left Odam. He felt that, losing Lilith, he was losing all. His thoughts began to rush with feverish speed.

"Lilith!" he cried, taking her hand. "The spirit of two is stronger than the spirit of one!"

It was merely an attempt to reassure her; he did not know as yet what could be done. But Lilith understood him differently.

"Yes, the spirit of two is strong," she agreed, and in the darkness he could see the wild spark in her eyes. "When a man and a woman want each other, they cannot be parted. We shall leave the tribe."

This decision came to Lilith suddenly. But in that instant everything turned firm in her—she was indomitable!

But Odam's breath stopped at this dreadful, sacrilegious thought. Had he ever heard of anyone leaving his tribe of his own will? The man of Tabunda belonged to the tribe from birth. He lived and died by its laws. But here, by Lilith's side, he was filled with giant courage: he was ready for even such a fearful sacrifice.

"Ag, we shall leave," he echoed in a choked voice.

They took apart the wall of the hut facing the forest and slipped out. At first they crept like snakes, then they ran, bent low, almost touching the ground with their hands. The light of the fire receded, the sound of the festive drum was scarcely audible now. Around them was the noise of the forest, ceaseless as the sound of waves breaking upon a rocky shore. Trees—dried out or killed by lightning—fell crashing behind them, their branches groaning as they caught at neighboring crowns. The terrifying, impenetrable dark was rent now and again with the howling of beasts and cries that made the heart sink: man is not made for night, he is the creature of day! At nightfall he must take cover in a shelter.

And yet they ran into the nocturnal forest, away from fire and safety. This must have been one of the first rebellions against that which is regarded as virtue. In the Tabunda tribe virtue, from time immemorial, was obedience to its customs, for customs kept people together and helped them to survive in the struggle with nature.

Odam and Lilith ran without halting, never going deep into the woods but also never coming out into open space. Dawn found them at the foot of the rocky mountain range. Trees grew in clusters—some on wide ledges, others on the sheer slopes, and then it seemed that they were standing head down.

The first rays of sunlight fell on barren cliffs; they turned brownish-red. The dazzling-white, almost square mountain that was visible from the encampment on the plain still dominated the range, but here it raised another giant shoulder. In its shelter, the valley of the little stream lay blissfully in the windless, warm air. But as soon as the current emerged from the valley, away from the protecting walls, the ground became barren, producing nothing but bitter grasses and sparse locust trees. And on the slopes there were only some scrawny, reddish shrubs.

Lilith and Odam sighed with relief at finding a semblance of shelter: the cave under the cliff would give them safety from wild beasts and cover from rain. They were hungry, but fatigue was uppermost. They stepped into the cave, dry and free of animal smells, and fell asleep at once, burying their faces in each other like children.

The blue sky flamed above them; innumerable insects buzzed and chattered in the grass; unfrightened lizards warmed themselves in the sun; birds and herbivorous animals lived their customary daytime lives. But Lilith and Odam did not wake till evening, and then only to build a fence in order to protect the entrance to the cave.

They drank from the nearby stream, finding it by the moisture in the air and the lushness of grass on its banks. Then they returned hurriedly to the shelter of the rocks. Twilight was falling—the most dangerous time of day. Without fire or weapons they did not dare to take a step.

They patiently endured hunger, although it was more than a day since they had eaten. But again they lay down silently on a bed of fresh grass, shyly touching each other with their fingers. So much had happened in so short a time that they did not know what to speak about, or how to speak. Their dreams were meager, but when they held each other's hands or touched each other with knees or shoulders, their inner currents seemed to be transmitted by the contact of warm skin—signals of friendliness, which reinforced the scanty language of words.

Large stars lit up the darkened sky. The air was filled again with growling and snorting and the sounds of the chase. It was the usual night of the wild forest, a time of fear, not love. Odam and Lilith lay still behind their fragile palisade. They spent several sleepless hours, keenly alert to every approaching sound. It was only before dawn that their instinct told them the danger was over, and they fell instantly asleep till morning.

And morning brought its own cares: they had to think of weapons and of food; their flight was ended. Now they were utterly alone, without support or help from anyone, like the first people on earth.

The earth was in its infancy. Its three faces were still smooth: the plow had not yet passed over the land, leaving the first wrinkles upon it; a ship's prow had not yet furrowed the serene waters; and the propeller of an airplane had not yet slit the air. But the joy of seeking was even then one of the most vital forces in man! It gave him a sense of the fullness of being. The first step inspired the second.

Man is a fearless creature, with great powers of endurance. In the struggle for existence that raged around him he was in his own element. Closeness to basic, simple laws—when killing is done for food and not out of hatred—formed his mind, resourceful but not cruel. An animal was not seen as an enemy; it was, rather, a fellow being which might save man from starving at a difficult time. When food was plentiful, man and his neighbors went their own ways without touching one another. The first totems might have appeared as expressions of gratitude rather than the wish to mollify the dreadful forces of nature. For people, in their own way, were thoroughly familiar with the world around them at the time. By following animal tracks they found water. Like birds, they slept in the trees. The world of rational and irrational creatures was not yet divided as sharply as today.

And man had already then formed a society that seems primitive to us now, and fleeting as a spark in the gray murk before the rising of the sun. But in reality it lasted for the longest period in history. Mankind, barely emerging, was making its first steps into communal living and laying the foundations for all that was to come. It was evolving speech and thought and the first glimmerings of culture, of technology, of medicine and art. And although it was small in numbers, what it was doing was to benefit generations undreamed of at the time.

The morning brought a rainstorm. Muddy streams ran down from the nearby mountains, carrying an avalanche of tumbling stones. Everything living hid itself. The watery sky covered the earth; the raindrops fell rapidly and densely, chattering like a host of insects all around. Then the cloud passed, and the air began to brighten. The gloom that had overwhelmed nature seemed to be flowing out through the gaps in the sky as more and more white and blue patches appeared in it. At last, a slanting ray of sunshine, newly washed, slid over the mossy rocks, and they began to steam. The earth glittered with small puddles. Trees, like wet animals, shook off the water.

Lilith and Odam stood at the cave entrance: the new world had cleansed itself to welcome them. They were happy.

But suddenly both were alert—they heard a light rustle. Under the trees, among the branches broken by the recent storm, a family of mountain goats was grazing. The dull-gray fur of the male almost merged with the gray tree trunks. His wide, powerful horns, like two crescent moons curving backward over his body, did not seem to burden his head at all. His muzzle turned to sniff the wind for hostile smells. The female and the kids grazed peacefully.

Odam clutched a knotty club—he had no other weapon then—and rushed out of concealment with a warlike cry.

"Ookhr! Ookhr!"

The goats darted away, toward the protecting rocks. An unequal race followed: the man did not know the terrain; the animals were escaping.

But Odam pursued them patiently, like all the hunters of Tabunda. He followed them until the raven, the bird of prophecy that looked like a charred log, with bluish whites around his proud dark eyes, flapped his sharp wing and cawed above him in a guttural undertone, as though purring in raven language. The hunting hours were over. The hot midday was at hand.

And when he was already climbing down the

slope, angered by failure, Odam suddenly stopped short: three steps away from him, in the fiery-hot, dense grass, a solitary goat, felled by the heat, was sleeping, his muzzle pressed against a rock, one crooked horn rising above his head.

Odam's muscles rolled like snakes under his skin. He dragged the first quarry he had overpowered without the help of his kinsmen home, to Lilith.

But when she ran to meet him, almost skipping, with that open loud laugh that Odam had loved since childhood, and butting his shoulder as if inviting him to gambol and celebrate the success together, he frowned and stepped back from her. What was good for love play was entirely inappropriate to the serious business of obtaining food.

He looked past her and walked to the spot where a fire was to be lit. The fire was a woman's task. Odam began to dress the animal as if he were alone. From early childhood he had seen all hunters do this, disregarding the praise and admiration showered upon them. Lilith stood puzzled. She was not yet offended by his first rebuff. She hesitated a mere second before turning to the age-old duties of a woman. But some portion of her joy went out of her heart.

On that day they feasted as never before. The animal was wholly theirs; there were no old people and no children to be given the choicest pieces.

They gorged themselves with liver and the delicate fat of the kidneys. They sucked the marrow from the bones and chewed the cartilage. They became intoxicated with the food and, retiring behind the fence, they left the glowing coals to frighten off nocturnal predators, attracted by man's tracks and the smell of blood on the ground.

In the dark, the former Odam returned to Lilith. Sated with food, they could not sate themselves with each other. Odam recalled the hunt; he was filled to the brim with the experience and with pride. Lilith prompted him whenever he could not find the needed words. She guessed even the things he could not recall, as though she herself had found the beast and, throwing the club at it, heard its surprised and painful death rattle.

Blissfully they fell asleep. The land of sleep differed little from their daytime world. They hunted, prepared food, sought shelter just as they did when awake. Nothing incomprehensible happened to them either in reality or in their dreams.

They had come to the grassy foothills with their clusters of trees at the most favorable season: fruits were ripening, shrubs were covered with berries, animals led their maturing young to the water holes. The sweet soft stems of springtime were no longer to be found, but the mealy roots and tubers were forming, and last year's nuts and acorns were still scattered everywhere under the trees. The summer promised to be happy and abundant.

The first movement of Lilith's fingers seemed almost purposeless; the bluish clay stretched softly, rounded out like a cloud changing its outlines in the wind. Lilith threw back her head. Her gaze slowly descended along the mountain slope, and the clay under her fingers turned into a mountain peak. Then instantly a tree trunk appeared on it. Then it became a goat, with horns curving over his back. Her glance no longer wandered; it concentrated on the crude torso, the bending hind legs. It was a likeness of the living animal, but so absurd! She wanted to destroy it at once.

But the animal was already moving, sniffing, threatening. Its color and its muscles played on its flanks. . . . And suddenly everything stopped: the animal strained forward, but did not disappear; it was running, but motionless!

Odam looked over her shoulder at the flat, moist cake of clay, the sharp stone in her muddy hands. A line ran down along the surface of the clay, and the contours of the head, back, forward leaping hooves appeared before the astonished Odam. He knew the piece of quartz she held; he had thrown it away as useless when he was chipping dartheads. Yet now the stone had turned out to possess strange powers— it captured yet another animal!

The clay dried, the drawing was hardening. Odam frowned and turned away. Lilith dropped her head, and the black wing of her hair hung down, covering her face. Odam slowly wandered off. That useless occupation—tracing clay with a rock—somehow disturbed, offended him. What did a woman need it for?

But Lilith did not follow him with her eyes. Her lips were parted, her nostrils flared, she continued to breathe in the odor of damp clay. She did not dare to touch the running line; the animal remained alive. She was afraid of frightening it off. At last, she threw her head back to take a deeper breath and saw the streaking silhouette of a bird in flight—the line of its outstretched head with the sharp beak, the sharp tail.

A sense of immense power flowed deep within her. She erased the running animal, smoothed the surface, and with the same stone she re-created in a few strokes—she herself did not know how—the vanished bird. It was impossible not to recognize it: the beak, the wings, the tail. . . . Lilith laughed. The departing Odam heard her laughter but did not glance back.

From the soft lump, returned to shapelessness, Lilith formed a human figure. Pensively she began to indicate the face, the hands. . . . Before her mind's eye stood her mother, who had lived only to the age of twenty-four. All the people of Tabunda died early. They were born with great powers of endurance, but once they fell ill, it was in vain that their relatives poured boiling water on the open wound, compelled the sick to sit before the fire for days, breathing the smoke, made them drink an acid potion brewed of ants.

Lilith's mother had gone to the other side of the world at dawn, when the last star quivered faintly in the sky—the star called the Heart of Day. Her body was tied to a log and floated down a forest river. The crying women shouted the tribe's funeral chant after her:

> *On the day of our death*
> *The wind comes*
> *To sweep away*
> *Our footprints. . . .*

The women sang:

> *For if it were not so,*
> *Then it would seem*
> *That we are still alive.*
> *That is why the wind comes*
> *To sweep away*
> *Our footprints.*

Her mother's narrow face with its prominent chin and full lips—the same pouting lips which in her daughter made the onlooker think of a ripe fruit that had been bitten into—her mother's face, long dead, her hair divided into two waves on either side of it, was never absent from Lilith's memory. The hollow cheeks, the high cheekbones, the glance forever flying forward—strange, how much and how little the daughter received from all this!

In the evenings, recalling her mother, Lilith looked at the stars. Raised in the woods, she could never become accustomed to their multitude and followed their flow patiently, silently, as though sinking her glance into a running stream.

But Odam remained indifferent to the sky. When the first star lit up, it was merely a signal that the nocturnal beasts would soon come out to hunt and that man's day was ended. Drowsiness closed his eyelids, he settled down more comfortably and fell asleep.

Lilith listened to the padding of soft paws, the thud of falling fruit, the owls' cries.

"Oa," she called softly.

Her young husband did not stir. Among many stars, one that grew larger and larger every night, as though someone were adding firewood to it, looked into his face. He paid it no attention.

Everything was strange Some thirst burned Lilith from within. The feeling was so formless and troubling that in the end it tired her and she would also fall asleep.

"What dreams are hanging on your lashes?" Odam would ask her in the morning, laughing.

Lilith knew that he did not believe her, that he was only teasing her, but she could not restrain herself: she had an overpowering need to fashion her vague dreams into words.

"One of the stars, the biggest in the sky, looked at your face last night," she began, and instantly noticed the grimace of displeasure on his lips. He did not like it when she entangled him in her imaginings. "You slept, and I wanted to rise higher. For the sky must be as hard as rock if it has so many fires on it. Then the star lowered its ray, and I caught at it as at a rope. . . ."

Odam involuntarily threw an anxious glance at her hand, as though it could still retain a mark of the silver knife blade of the star. But instantly he flew into anger both at himself and at Lilith. For he divided all phenomena into two kinds: those that he knew—and then he knew them very well, he knew if they were edible, hostile, dangerous, useful—and those he did not know, did not need, and was not threatened by. These he simply never thought about. No, he had no intention to listen to Lilith's tales, afraid to yield to her in anything, even inwardly. If he yielded, he felt, he would be left without any point of support; he would be whirled away down the current of different thoughts and images, which he could not foresee or understand and which he therefore instinctively avoided.

In the mornings he would go off in search of stones for an ax and spearheads. The stone had to be damp, fresh, not dried out by the sun. Odam knew that such stones were dug up from the earth; but maybe they could also be split off from a layer of rock, and then he could collect the sharp splinters.

Lilith remained all day near the cave. She dug a small hollow to serve as a hearth and spread a layer of clay on the ceiling of the cave above it. That was when she had first discovered that clay can be stretched, lending the lump a variety of shapes. It was her own discovery. The people of Tabunda did not make clay pots; they used ox bladders, shells, hollowed wood, sewn leather, and closely woven baskets as containers. Gradually Lilith accumulated a full set of household utensils. Odam gave her a present—a slate knife, wide, with a hole drilled in it so that she could hang it on her belt.

In the vicinity of the cave she set out snares for small animals and gathered acorns, which she later ground with a stone pestle. To bake flatcakes, she would dig a round hole, heat stones at the bottom of it, and cover them with a thick layer of leaves. The flattened dough was again covered with leaves and a layer of earth, on which she then would make a fire. In the morning she would have well-baked bread, sometimes with a stuffing of berries, fish, or earthworms, and they would eat it all to the last crumb.

For the first time Odam and Lilith owed nothing to anyone. They suddenly found themselves free, utterly free of anything, or anyone.

This made Odam worry. Instinctively he still looked around him: if there were no people nearby, then perhaps he could find at least a totem—some strange rock or a tree or an unknown animal that he could cling to in spirit. But Lilith dreamed of a new

sun lighting up above them, different from the sun
of the Tabunda tribe. Would it be hotter, or dimmer?
That would be as they deserved.

Odam held on to what he knew. He still had no
models for comparison. No experience of ages guided
him. He clung to the crumbs of his former knowledge
as naturally as Lilith overstepped the old.

When Odam returned from the hunt, she would
dash headlong for fresh water to the river, which was
shallow and warm. And suddenly she would stop to
watch a flock of sky-blue fish. She would step into the
water and follow them until the water reached her
lips or until Odam, after waiting vainly by the cave,
would come calling her and searching for her.

She would come out on the bank shamefaced,
water streaming down her hair, her hands empty. For
she did not hunt fish, she merely looked at them.

Winter and summer months rolled over them like
small and large waves, falling away, dissolving. The
sense of time existed in Odam and Lilith, but its
precise count would not begin until much later.

Although the language of the Tabunda tribe was
meager, almost everything around had already been
named by man: trees were called trees, and water—
water. Yet specialization was selective. Many predators awakened in the forest at nightfall and set out,
roaring, in search of quarry. But if they did not
threaten man, why should he concern himself with
them? The edible roots occasionally found by Lilith

had no names either; she only remembered food she found often: sour roots, sweet berry, bitter leaf.

It was a time of furious word-making! Almost every day brought something new. Lilith and Odam followed the flow of their associations. Some of the words remained in memory, but most of the time they flared up and went out like sparks. A familiar thing would suddenly present itself in a new aspect and be given a new name. The sky could be bright; or watery when it rained; or terrifying when it thundered. To us, though different at different times, the sky invariably remains "the sky." But Lilith's contemporaries saw separate elements in it, often disparate and hostile to one another: the terrifying sky devoured the bright one like an immense maw. But then it was defeated in turn by the watery sky. And, washed clean by the streaming rain, it returned to man's eyes friendly, cloudless, and blue.

Lilith and Odam used many verbs, which revolved around daily needs. But words like "eat," "drink," "hide," or "smell" were never general. Each time the verb was concrete: "to drink water from the cold stream," "to hide from the shaggy beast," "to smell the odor of the tree that grows alone."

Lilith and Odam lived more in the world of smells than those of colors and sounds. They not only felt them keenly but became passionately fond of them. Lilith rubbed herself with wild dill; she gathered wormwood; she dried balsamic roots.

The word "love" did not exist in the Tabunda language. The power of attraction was expressed in special words, unlike any preserved in modern languages. Death was described by metaphors: "to go to the other side of the world," "to flow away with the water." Sleep was adjacent to death. Dreams were the lifting of the edge of mystery. They were like intimations of something beyond the mountains: the idea of the beautiful, somewhere far away, has always existed in the mind of man.

But it would be vain to seek moral concepts in the language of Tabunda. Good and bad were determined by strength. Sorrow, regret, memories—all these existed, but men were not yet able to name them.

Odam was getting ready for the hunt. For several days they had been unsuccessful—their traps remained empty. The stocks of food collected by Lilith had been exhausted. Besides, the unfamiliar tracks of some large animal had appeared in the vicinity. Was it this animal that frightened off their quarry? Before dawn, Odam concealed himself not far from the path to the watering place, and when the first glints of the sun had risen from behind the purple rocks, he caught sight of a tiger's back, with stripes like reeds. The animal moved lightly, silently, sniffing the ground. Finally, convinced that he was safe, the tiger lay down on the stony riverbed, partly exposed now by the drought. His front paws were wide, powerful, reddish-golden; his hind ones were thinner, with narrow stripes across them. He lapped the water in the shallow stream, and when he had had enough, he yawned and scraped his claws over the rock. Then he rose lazily and walked away along the stream. For some days after that, Odam and Lilith were afraid to leave their cave, but the tiger's tracks had not appeared again in the nearby area.

And now Odam hurried to replenish his stock of weapons. With the aid of a stone chipper, he split off narrow, sharp layers from a piece of flint. He had learned to do this with a single stroke. Beside him there was already a pile of slivers ready to be used as knives, hole-makers, and spearheads. Lilith, meantime, was scratching a dying bull on a dart—a token of success in the coming hunt. The ornamentation, which would seem to us to be no more than a jumble of slanted lines, represented the hunter's strength and luck: his spears and darts were to fly as thick and fast as rain! And then where could the animal escape? The hungry Lilith poured into her art all of her perseverance, all her desire for Odam's success.

But soon she seemed to forget the purpose of her work. Her animal was powerful! He walked across the plain with horned head bent slightly forward. The wind carried a multitude of smells toward him, and Lilith's nostrils flared unwittingly. Her hand holding the sharp stone scraper dropped of itself upon her knees. Her veiled glance moved over the objects around her. A flower swayed in the breeze nearby. Bees crept into its wide calyx; the flower buzzed from within. And Lilith threw her hair back from her ear, listening. She was oblivious of the flow of time, sunny and summery. . . .

Lilith believed in her animal—the little bull painted with ochre. She ought to have shown him dying, but he still walked and walked upon the plain without sensing danger. And Lilith suddenly began to draw little broken lines around him—the rustling grasses! They smelled of honey and satiety. They gave life to the red-furred beast. . . .

She started because Odam had called her. He had done it reluctantly: a man should not address a woman before going out to hunt. No, she had never become a diligent wife, this Lilith, whom he had sought so stubbornly. Instead of offering him the dart without speaking, she sat and dreamed of something, staring before her. He was becoming increasingly irritated at this idleness, and even more so at his need to seek her aid; for he himself would never have been able to scratch even the feeblest likeness of an animal on his weapons.

Without looking, he took the dart from her and slipped it into his quiver with the others. Lilith knew that this charmed dart would fly at the most crucial moment, and she felt guilty foreseeing failure; she had drawn an animal that had escaped, not one brought down! And this was how it would be.

She followed Odam with her eyes for a long time, meekly promising him in her mind that she would go at once far up into the mountains to gather honey of the mountain bees, set out some snares for rodents, or search for a nest with fledgling birds.

The forest growing near the cave climbed over the hill. Lilith halted at the edge of the ravine; here it was still possible to walk around it. The clay slope began as an innocuous hollow, the roots of the trees stretching across it like a bridge. And at the bend, a bright rivulet seeped out directly from the ground. Lilith bent over it and drank. The water was tart, it prickled her tongue. In a tiny cascade, the rivulet plunged down and disappeared among the roots, then reemerged ten paces lower as a creek. It did not hiss or gurgle—it was still too small for that.

Lilith forgot what she had come for. She no longer felt hungry, she was consumed with curiosity. She drank again as she climbed down the hill, but the ravine grew steeper, and she had to clutch at branches and tufts of grass to keep her balance. The water was gathering force—she could already wet her feet in it. Soon it rose to her ankles. Lilith walked and walked as though bewitched; she was shaken by a sudden realization—it was the river! The river that flowed across the plain. This was its source. She, Lilith, Daughter of Night, was seeing the birth of a river.

Vague thoughts possessed her. If the river had a beginning, it must also end somewhere, as the forest did. And where was the end of the white mountain that touched the sky? . . . Her thoughts broke off. She was tired. She felt hunger again.

Lilith stepped out of the water and climbed up the slope, higher and higher, past the sticky, fragrant trees dressed in needles like hedgehogs. Yellowish-gray lizards with brown patterns on their backs scurried underfoot. She managed to strike one with a stone and roasted it in a fire of dry rhododendron twigs. Around her, ranunculi opened wide their enormous purple cups. On the northern slope grew violet daisies. But, of course, she had no name for them.

The air became dryer and colder, but small islands of warmth still remained under the trees. Lilith stopped from time to time under a tree to warm herself. In the distance she caught sight of something white with uneven edges. As always when she met the unexpected, Lilith halted but did not retreat. The white spot did not move; it was not likely to be anything alive. There was something calming, reassuring in its color.

Lilith came nearer, squatted down, and touched it. Her finger encountered something cold. She stepped on it with her foot: it cracked like an eggshell. Through the breach she saw some stiff blades of grass. She scooped up a handful of the brittle shell, but was astonished to find it soft and weightless and disappearing as she looked. Her hands became wet, and there was nothing left!

On the ground, however, the shell remained. Lilith backed away, rounded the brittle white spot, and continued to climb. But for a long time she kept glancing back at it. There were more and more white spots as she went on. They lay so silently, gleaming in the sun! Her feet sank deeper and deeper into them. A vague intimation flashed through Lilith's mind: the high mountain rising like a motionless cloud over the valley must consist entirely of this crisp and fluffy stuff! But now her feet were chilled, and she had enough good sense not to climb any higher.

This was truly a day of wonders: she had made discovery after discovery and luckily escaped all dangers.

A little earlier she had caught sight in a clearing of a hunting python, its body covered with black and yellow patterns. The people of Tabunda valued snake-skin. It was used to sheathe the quivers that held the hunters' darts; women sewed strips of it into their festive clothing.

But an encounter with a huge snake could mean death. Lilith hid behind a thorny juniper shrub. The python's small graceful head that resembled a flower on a stem was raised, and its narrow tongue flicked rapidly. Before it sat a little animal, paralyzed with fright. The python drew itself nearer and nearer to its victim. Its red eyes—who knows what they were seeing at this moment and what they neglected to see!—burned fixedly on either side of its head.

And suddenly, the unforeseen. An enemy pounced on the snake—a slender-bodied little predator with tail raised high in warlike fashion. The reptile tossed violently, trying to throw off the attacker. But the sharp teeth gripping the back of its neck would not relax.

Lilith did not wait to see the outcome of the struggle. She crept up to the petrified hare which had never recovered from its hypnotic state, killed it with a stone, and, slinging it over her shoulder as her legitimate quarry, made off with it.

Hurrying back, she lost the way.

The day was ending. Lilith felt anxious and walked with springy, almost flying steps. The land seemed to be lower now. Rocks extruded from the mountainside. Among them curled shrubs of dewberry with ripening fruit.

Suddenly she came upon a viscous yellow rivulet that ran along the dry ground, curving around anthills. She dipped the end of a stick in it and brought it to her lips. It was wild honey, overflowing from a beehive in the hollow of a tree—an unexpected boon. Lilith dropped to her knees and sipped the rare delicacy. When she had had enough, she sought out the hollow, and with her shale knife she cut out as many honeycombs as she had room for in her shoulder basket.

The day was dying rapidly. Lilith climbed back again to a higher, safer place with bare rocks. A low-growing pine, as scrawny and bent as a hunchback, rustled its branches—a ceaseless, dreary sound. Lilith collected fallen leaves and twigs, gathered up some sand to form a little mound, and settled down for the night among the pine roots. The fur of the dead rabbit gave her a little warmth. She was afraid to make a fire.

Hour after hour, now dozing off, now waking, she waited for the dawn. After a long while, gray clouds like a tangled web began to swirl and breathe over the mountains. The mountains themselves were still invisible, they were just about to emerge from the predawn murk.

The laminated rocks and the soft earth seemed to be the sole realities; clouds flew overhead like dense rain, the cupola of the sky leaned sideways drunkenly. It might have been the time of the division of the firmament from the waters.

The deadly cold pierced Lilith to the bone. The wind touched her lips. But her breath came free and proud: the whole world lay at her feet! And it was small now, with ragged spots of woods and barrens.

Birds, awakening, burst into song. The struggle of the mountaintop and darkness was over.

Suddenly the sun's fiery disk broke out of the grayness. It was plain and solitary, without a single ray—like the head of a mushroom rising from the ashes of last night's fire.

Lilith leaped up and raised her arms, still numb with the night's chill.

"Loo! I see thee, sun!"

She had never been in this place before. A narrow mountain lake lay in the glade beneath her. In the evening, veiled with fog, its banks merged with the water. But in the morning the water was clear, greenish-gray. Hundreds of dead multicolored butterflies littered the shore. Not a single fish plashed in the lake. Lilith approached the water and bent over it. The bottom seemed bloody. She stepped into the water, which barely reached her knees, and pulled out a lump of something hard, with coarse facets. It was red. After a moment's hesitation, Lilith licked it —and cried out with joy. Salt! What could be more precious?

Now she no longer hurried home. She had to weave a sack first. And while she was filling the sack with her rich find, something extraordinary happened.

There was a strange, measured crackling, a steady hum overhead. Lilith raised her face. The sky was strewn with white shells; tiny cloudlets swayed like a reflection in the water. And large gray eggs fell from the sky. As they approached the earth, they grew enormous.

Lilith dashed for the safety of rocks and shrubs. The sack, the lumps of salt, the basket with the honeycombs remained on the bank.

The gray giants settled softly on the water, moved up close to the bank, and the smooth shell of one of them opened up a little, without cracking as a bird's egg would, and released a curious creature from its bowels. . . .

The same thing happened with the second and the third egg.

Lilith mechanically counted the odd creatures who emerged from the eggs by the twenty-five unit count used by the Tabunda tribe: the little finger, the fourth, which was nameless, the middle, the index, the thumb. . . . If she continued, she would have gone on to the wrist, the shoulder, the collarbone, the earlobe, the temple, the crown, and again—the temple, the earlobe, the collarbone. . . . The system employed by the tribe permitted counting to a considerable number.

But there were only five eggs, and five creatures had come out of them. Lilith did not doubt for a second that those were living beings before her. For they had descended from above; they had not come out of the forest thickets, where the spirits of the dead depart together with the water. She had never thought about it before, but why should people and animals not live up there, among the stars and clouds?

Yet it was terrifying. She was afraid to betray herself by the least movement, and she waited, immobile as a lizard, among the rocks.

Lilith's sharp eyes were not all-seeing. Her glance slipped thoughtlessly over the ores extruding on the surface of the rocks; falling water called forth no thoughts about motion; cereal grasses ripened vainly in the valleys. Man went his way on earth so lightly, stole along so cautiously, that nature barely noticed his presence. And he knew nothing at all of the great forces all about him.

Lilith dashed headlong till she heard ringing blows, repeated by a thousand echoes: Odam was toiling with his ax in the sweat of his brow.

The sound of splitting wood seemed ordinary, human, and Lilith halted to catch her breath. The strange, high-pitched hum, the clicking and snapping that had struck her at the lake almost as much as the appearance of the astonishing beings that seemed to move purposefully and kept turning their terrifying heads with bulging eyes in her direction—all this was gradually dissolving at the peaceful sight of the familiar forest and the sound of the ax. The excellent stone ax over which Odam had labored five dawns.

Lilith's cheeks were burning, she was breathing heavily. Before approaching Odam, whose bowed body she already saw among the tree trunks, she halted to collect herself. She did not know how to describe what she had seen. The beings were neither birds nor animals. They did not look like her and Odam, although she tended to associate them with herself rather than with animals.

Her intense concentration led her to attempt to understand the event through images, through phenomena similar in appearance or in substance. Poetry is the primal effort to unshackle the muteness of thought. And Lilith had encountered the inexpressible.

"Odam," she said. "Beyond the mountains men have come down from the sky in eggs. Their bodies are dressed in turtle shells, but even stronger. They have shiny round heads, like fish. Over the tops of their heads they have ant whiskers. And they fly like birds."

Odam needed a long time before the meaning of her words could reach him. Then he straightened up and looked in the direction she was pointing. His hand involuntarily reached for his sling.

But the mountains were far, the woods serene. He breathed a sigh of relief.

"Fish don't fly," he said.

FROM LAOLA-LYAL

"Every step in the realm of cognition
Entails an equal step
Of self-denial."

THE PLANET of Laola-Lyal lay in the eighth vertical of the fifth outer circle of a small galaxy in the zone of violet displacement. No human measure could define its distance from Earth in terms of moving light. The distance was too great.

In the zone of violet displacement the forces of gravitation are stronger: galaxies are drawn together. More matter is concentrated within a given space, and the cohesion within it is greater. In the zone of red displacement, the zone of the young, expanding galaxies, the situation is quite different. This was the first light-message received from outer space by Laola-Lyal and decoded by its scientists. Subsequent messages introduced correctives into their computations concerning the planet's future.

They also learned that the galaxy to which their planet belonged had been created artificially by another, dying civilization. Completing its own cycle, that civilization had fulfilled the duty of all life: it produced a likeness of itself. In order to bequeath this duty to future intelligent life in the new galaxy, it had launched a signal satellite into a complex predetermined orbit. By the time the younger galaxy was completing its period of violet displacement, the signal satellite was to be drawn into its gravitational sphere and start revolving around its inhabited planet, attracting the attention of the intelligent beings on it.

The light impulses the signal satellite sent forth

were based on a system of numbers. They were to explain the secret of the galaxy's origin, as well as warn of its impending end. Thus it would perhaps lead to a repetition of the earlier experiment: a second launching of a nucleus of energy that would develop into yet another artificial galaxy.

And so the scientists of Laola-Lyal discovered that their galaxy had long entered the zone of violet displacement, the zone of contraction, and was undeviatingly moving toward its end—toward that great center of compressed primal matter which, like a giant cauldron, both shoots out newborn galaxies into space and draws into itself the galaxies that have completed their destined trajectories. Such is the vortex of eternal destruction and renewal in one of the innumerable corners of the stellar universe.

All of this had been decoded by several generations of scientists on Laola-Lyal. And they conceived a daring, unprecedented idea—not merely to bequeath to the future the germ of an artificial new galaxy but also to save their own civilization! To transfer it to suitable planets in the zone of red displacement— the zone of youth!

They wanted not only to repeat the eternal cycle of development but also to attempt to reach beyond it. Transferred to a young planet, the civilization of Laola-Lyal would continue to exist in time. And then perhaps it would at last succeed in building a bridge into the antiworld.

The Laolitans would teach the younger beings of planets in the red light galaxies what they had already achieved; they would shorten their paths to knowledge. And who could tell what new perspectives might open up before the combined intelligence of beings developing within the same key of cognition, regardless of their outer appearance!

However, for over a century this idea had been only a tempting dream. There had been no practical means of accomplishing the evacuation: the speed of light rays was clearly insufficient for the task, since all speeds, including that of light, are subject to the curve of space. In a world of complex gravitations it is impossible to draw a straight line between two points. The line will inevitably bend under the impact of gravitational forces.

And the scientists wondered: could the crux of the problem lie in the gravitational "mass" of the body itself? A stone thrown into outer space deforms the straight line of its flight. Even the speed of light is powerless to break the bonds of gravitation in the universe. . . . The universe? Or perhaps only in their own Metagalaxy? Could other laws, of different physics, possibly prevail among the other great Stellar Islands?

And so a new idea was born and was named hypothetically Movement Along the Chord. It was proven that Movement Along the Chord would "break through" the curve of space, bringing the spacecraft into other vastnesses, where speed was entirely un-limited.

However, the attempt to put this theory into prac-tice could destroy the craft! Within the limits of the Metagalaxy, velocities above the speed of light annihilate matter. And yet . . . hadn't the Laolitans learned already in the distant past to control the chain reaction of both atomic fission and synthesis in time?

And one of the scientists of Laola-Lyal came for-ward with the mind-staggering theory of "chain an-nihilation."

Even the rational Laolitans, accustomed to many marvels, gasped at the daring notion. An extraordi-nary thing happened: the atavistic fear of the new awakened in them. Freedom of ideas, which had long become a law, was shaken: the many attacked the one. And yet . . .

The grandiose plan of resettlement could not be accomplished by the resources of the planet's econ-omy without a stringent reduction in the living standard. Long accustomed to abundance, the Laoli-tans had to assume a life of voluntary limitation to bare essentials and devote all their means and energies for at least a thousand years to the distant and uncertain future. An enormous sacrifice! They hesitated. They had attained so much, and the pre-dicted destruction of their planet was still almost half a million years away!

Nevertheless, gradually infusing the minds of several generations, the idea of resettlement had won out. Movement Along the Chord had come to be regarded as the greatest discovery of all time, a discovery that could be relayed to other worlds. It wrought a radical change in the thinking of the Laolitans. It excited them with the possibility of bringing together intelligent beings of different stellar systems.

Nearly all the resources of Laola-Lyal were poured into the sending of expeditions to young galaxies of the red displacement zones in various corners of the universe. These journeys of unimaginable distances —for the time being no more than blind probes— could bring the Laolitans to planets with intelligent life of altogether different forms and structures. But the explorers were not allowed any time for detailed study or investigation. Their task was merely to search for planets with colloidal structures and suitable oxygen conditions, which could subsequently be adapted and modified, if need be.

The problem, moreover, involved not only the sending of living explorers into the depths of space but also the transmitting of information to the home planet without long delays. Otherwise, because of the enormous stretches of time, the whole enterprise might become meaningless: the cosmonauts and Laola-Lyal would be living unrelated lives, devoid of fruitful communication.

Information was relayed back to Laola-Lyal by means of special automatic carrier systems. As they traveled, they developed faster-than-light speeds, speeds at which atoms of matter are completely altered in structure, reaching a state of supercompression similar to that of the center of the Metagalaxy, that eternally bearing womb of the universe.

As they approached Laola-Lyal—and this was carefully computed in advance and set to occur at intervals of sixty planetary years—the data carriers slowed down to a normal, sublight velocity. The restoration of the atoms to their former state was achieved with the aid of a special galactic generator devised by the Laolitans.

By the time the Nameless One was born (this was the name given by Lilith to the second Laolitan to emerge from the flying egg at the Salt Lake as she counted them on her fingers), the life of Laola-Lyal had already been subjected to the needs of cosmic exploration for over three centuries. Yet the task was still in the stage of the Great Search—of intergalactic reconnaissance. For it was clear by now that the resettlement of the entire planet could not be accomplished by the resources of Laola-Lyal alone. It could succeed only if the inhabitants of other planets came to its aid by supplying the ships of the celestial navigators with raw materials for energy production.

The Nameless One was no longer young when he reached the Earth. His craft had followed the circles of the Universe for a long time. Long enough to store up in the traveler's mind the memory of many stellar worlds. But had the Nameless One ever given any thought to himself?

In his early youth he had lived for a time on an artificial platform two hundred thousand kilometers from his planet. There were four scientists on duty, and they served in six-month shifts. They had easy contact with the home planet, and time passed quickly. Each man conducted his own observations. They would gradually become accustomed to the black sky with its shaggy sun, devoid of any red, and the vast numbers of luminaries which never set and never dimmed. The sight, however, brought them no pleasure.

The Nameless One had grown up on a well-organized planet at the height of its development. His world had been ruled by logic and the thirst for knowledge. Man had been freed of all anxieties connected with his daily life and safety. Civilization was no longer regarded as a means toward increased comforts; needs had long been reduced to a minimum; the only thing that remained unlimited was the opportunity to develop one's own gifts. The most perfect discipline reigned on the planet: the discipline of understanding. Such concepts as rebellion, individualism, or personal power had long gone out of existence.

At the same time, every Laolitan was constantly

aware of his strong bond with the others. He knew
his exact place in society; he never doubted the use-
fulness of his labor. And he knew that, should the
need arise, Laola-Lyal would bring all of its mighty
resourses to his aid. For each individual was an
active part of society, and no one existed merely on
his own.

Long before the end of his shift on the space
platform, the Nameless One had been summoned
home by an unexpected raygram. His comrades were
excited and slightly envious—he was returning to
the world of daylight! But their envy contained no
element of ill will. There was no ground for such feelings among the Laolitans. Each performed his
allotted task, and none was singled out above the
others.

The Nameless One was given the most precise
time coordinates. He must not err by the slightest
fraction of a second, or he would not be able to land
at the designated point.

The work of the space platform was concerned
with problems of gravitation; hence the method of
travel selected was gravitational. It was somewhat
slower, but it would provide further data for the
instruments.

His companions checked all the systems, attached
the feed lines to all the connecting and regulating
devices, and now the Nameless One, dressed in a
strong and bulky space suit, with his helmet firmly

secured, stood ready for the flight at the edge of the platform. His hand in the inflated glove rested lightly on the rail. All he had to do was step out into space, into the black infinity.

It was not a pleasant moment. The atavistic terror of the abyss retained its hold in some tiny cell of consciousness. However, the Nameless One's attention was centered on the time signal. The moment it came, he let go of the rail and stepped into emptiness. The artificial gravitation of the platform no longer held him, and he was fully in the power of the gravitational forces of Laola-Lyal.

He had studied the planet well from the space station, for its large disk covered a substantial area of the dark sky. Now he slowly began to approach it. So slowly that at first it seemed to his comrades he was merely suspended in space. They could see his face clearly through the transparent helmet. He was smiling.

They stood a little longer at the edge, waved to him, and dispersed, each to his own task. He had ceased to be part of their group, having been given his own separate assignment.

About two hours later, one of them looked out and was astonished to see the Nameless One still so near. He waved again, and the Nameless One answered.

The hours designated as nighttime set in on the platform. He also dozed inside his shell. The instruments showed that the gravitational forces were steadily increasing his speed, but he was not aware of this himself. The giant disk of the planet might have grown larger after a day's journey; to him it seemed the same. He merely distinguished its continents somewhat more clearly; the cloud cover shifted in different places, and flat areas were transformed into reliefs. That was all. And yet he flew quite rapidly. The entire journey was meant to last eight planetary days. Of course, a light-plane could have made it in one minute, but his instruments were gathering information. Gravitational flights were of special interest at the moment. His only regret was that he had to remain idle. Only the automatic devices were active; he seemed to have been turned into a mere stuffing for the space suit.

It was perhaps wrong of him to have such thoughts, but the black emptiness irritated him. Besides, for the first time in his life, something was left unclear: he had not been told the reason for his summons. Everything done by the people of Laola-Lyal was done rationally and voluntarily. The very term "obedience" was absent from the language. And this call without any explanation inevitably stung his pride.

To the flier in space it seems that he is the center of the universe. On all sides he is surrounded by equidistant vastness, as though he were at the heart of a giant black sphere.

He flew through emptiness, occasionally slipping

down the helmet shield over his face to rest from the
sight of the glimmering lights of the cosmos. At
other times he idly scanned his native planet, dreaming of the coming meeting with the woman who was
to have become the mother of his child by the time
of his return.

But now the Nameless One was coming back much
sooner. He wondered whether she knew. She did not
like the unexpected.

Of the three women he had loved, the first remained the most distant from him—the Laolitan
Likhé. And yet he sometimes thought that, in his last
hours, it would be her calm, trusty hand that he
would long to touch.

She had never been wholly his; she belonged to no
one. Love occupied so small a place in her life that
he often felt awkward and superfluous, as though
he was distracting her from something more important. She was never saddened by their frequent sepa-
rations and never awaited reunion with too much
warmth. She had decided to have their child after
sober thought and only after examinations by the
embryologist and geneticist confirmed that the com-
pletion of her physical development required it.

She was well trained, absolutely healthy, and even-
tempered in all her relationships. As even as a road
on which no accidents, no chance encounters could
ever happen.

And yet he loved her timidly and fiercely. He had
to watch himself constantly, lest he betray his secret
tenderness. He dreaded her ridicule. She turned the
divine gift of laughter into a punishing scourge. To
her, everything was an occasion for mockery, never
for warmth or sadness. Was she intelligent? Oh, yes,
very! Was she kind? "And what does that mean?"

They had met at a student club in early spring.
Likhé was already then intensely absorbed in the
theory of cybernetic immortality. The field of radiation of psychic activity had been just recently discovered and needed theoretical elaboration. There
were many questions to be answered. What happened
to man's psychic energy after death? During the
disintegration of matter? The brain, that storehouse
of information, was absolutely material. There was
nothing mystical in its radiations. Like all other
waves, brain waves were capable of moving in space
regardless of their source. In other words, they
seemed to have independent existence once they
were emitted.

"Can we assume," Likhé spoke in a hypnotically
even voice, "that the universe—no, not merely our
galaxy, but the entire universe, which is still beyond
the reach of our investigative mechanisms—is built
according to a unified, rational plan? If this is so,
then the appearance of rational beings can be said
to serve a specific purpose: they are the scouts on the
peripheries of creation. The meaning of their lives

lies in the accumulation of data concerning their environment."

The Nameless One did not think so. He followed a different philosophy, which considered nature a mere arena of chance. But he did not interrupt Likhé— both out of a sense of delicacy and out of a desire to go on listening to her voice.

They were sitting on the grass, in a remote corner of the forest sanctuary. The day was slipping into evening. The fading light was filtering through the dense foliage of tall shrubs. The sunset sky was bluish-purple. There was more blue than pink in it. The flame of enormous energies unfolded and bloomed like a giant flower.

Likhé reclined, her head resting on her hand. Her wrists were brittle, her movements small and quick. Her eyes were strange. There was something piercing in them. They punctured and stung—and yet she did not mean to hurt. Her glance was like a signal from another planet—it came across vast distances. It was eternally in flight. It could almost be touched . . . but it was not yet here.

To the Nameless One, Likhé remained a being forever elusive, never really known or understood, although he had become her husband that very evening. When the brief twilight deepened and the moons came up, each in its own phase, they had involuntarily drawn closer together. At first he had felt no excitement. Her head leaned trustingly against his shoulder. But then one of the moons had thrown a sheaf of silvery-purple light upon her face, her closed eyes—and ancient forces flared up in both.

Afterwards, contrary to custom and common sense, they did not want to part. They even had to make some sacrifices, although the heaviest burden fell to the Nameless One. It was he who had stayed with Likhé. Of his two professions, he had to choose the one he liked least—that of a doctor. But this permitted him to work in the same laboratory with her.

Nevertheless, he remained critical of her search for a single mental field, into which the radiations of the human brain supposedly flowed after death. He was repelled by the concept of immortality as an immense repository of impersonal information. To him, the most precious aspects of being were the irrational, the subconscious, his troubling love for Likhé, his aching sense of kinship with the land, the plants, and the few remaining animals of Laola-Lyal. It was from these that he drew the inner certitudes, the values that were to govern his future development.

He became so tired of the "cybermentalists," as he disrespectfully dubbed them in his own mind, that after a year he rebelled and decided to change his occupation. Now he was able to see Likhé only from time to time. However, on Laola-Lyal most of the men and women lived like that. Marriage had long ceased to bind them to a common home. Likhé, busy, absorbed, ever ready to mock any emotional impulse but invariably truthful and reliable, remained his wife. A mysterious being behind seven veils!

Often he would speak to her silently: "My dear Likhé, my clever Likhé, please don't say anything, and don't smile. Let me retain at least a vestige of illusion that you need me."

When she decided to have a child, she told him about it quite simply. To her, this act did not hold any elements of mystery. The laboratory tests of their genes took about a week. Both knew precisely the moment of conception. That night, no room was left for anything even remotely resembling love.

Everything augured well for Likhé's pregnancy. The work at the Mental Research Center had been reduced to economize energy for the coming inter-galactic expeditions. And now Likhé was free to carry and bear the child without breaking any medical rules.

The Nameless One intended to spend those months with her, when he was suddenly invited to take part in the next tour of duty on the gravitational cosmic platform. This was, in a sense, a test, a means of selecting personnel for future distance flights.

Likhé was delighted that he had been chosen for the test even before he had had time to decide whether he wanted to go. She would have been ex-tremely surprised had he refused. And he avoided surprising her: it seemed to him that she regarded him more and more soberly after each surprise.

And so it happened that he was assigned directly from the gravitational platform to the crew of an expedition to the Milky Way. The preparations took only two years. His daughter was still a baby when Likhé came with her to see him off at the cosmodrome. He was tormented by the thought that his daughter would grow up, get old, and possibly die before his ship had reached its very first objective. And he would still be only twenty-four years old.

His wife seemed restless during the final hours at the cosmodrome. The ship had not yet risen, but they were far apart now, as if inwardly she had already said good-bye to him. And although he was destined to survive by unimaginable ages not only her but also his remote descendants, the great-great-grandchildren of the tiny girl stirring in her mother's arms, whose baby smell was still on his lips, he felt that Likhé was facing a life far richer than his would ever be. He had no doubt that she would soon find a replacement for him and be as happy as she had been with him.

But he—he faced an almost immortal love. Memories fed by loneliness.

When for a short time he loved another woman, Elil, whom he had met on a distant, alien planet, it seemed to him that he had simply transferred to her all the reserves of his unexpended love for Likhé. The daughter born to him there had also assumed the lineaments of the child left far behind. And it was only after he had been obliged to leave them, too, losing them in the irreversible abyss of time, that he had gradually come to realize how dear they were to him, how much he loved them—for themselves, and not as mere reflections of the others, the half-forgotten ones. And then, tormented by regret, by the impossibility to redeem his guilt, to look at them again with different, wide-open eyes, he painfully relived in memory his fragile happiness.

GREEN BOWL

THE GREEN BOWL PLANET belonged to the Equinoctial Galaxy. It had reached the verge of violet displacement but had not yet crossed into it. Green Bowl—a lovely lake that glistened from the cosmic distance like a polished mirror—was far from being the happiest of places. All the efforts of its population were directed at drying and cooling the planet: a stray bolide, presumably of antimatter, had collided with the planet a thousand years before. It had melted the polar caps, flooded the continents in a universal deluge, and, worst of all, disrupted the biosphere. The forests had been covered with water and ceased to release oxygen. The excess of carbon dioxide had overheated the body of the planet like a cotton-wool lining. The planet sweated and struggled with all-pervasive mold. The intense radiation had killed most of the animals; others were stimulated to develop in new forms.

The remnants of the human population, helped by the populations of two other planets of the galaxy, directed all their efforts into saving this suffocating, half-dead planet. In the course of several centuries, mighty forests were developed on the mountainsides. With great speed they "gobbled" the carbon dioxide and grew like mushrooms after rain. The excess heat was forcibly extracted from the ocean and the stifling atmosphere and transformed into energy. Energy was so abundant that Green Bowl readily offered to share it with future settlers.

The "ore field" of the ocean was also enormously rich: mollusks accumulated copper; medusas, zinc and lead. The "water culture" of Green Bowl, reversing all preceding history, opened entirely new perspectives. The resources of the water completely replaced those of the land.

The soil, formerly impoverished by reckless tilling, was now freed of the task of providing food. The population nourished itself by cultivating fields of marine plants. Sea water—nutrient for plankton—contained everything needed by living organisms for the formation of their bones and shells, muscles and blood. This marine food, with its high phosphorus, calcium, and protein content enriched the brains of the planet's residents, transforming them mentally and morally.

It was a remarkable planet, covered with illimitable, deeply breathing seas. It was called Green Bowl, and the word "green" became synonymous with "beautiful."

The Nameless One took a long time getting accustomed to its glitter, its vast, bare distances, and its pervasive sense of the kinship of all living beings before the face of the silent waters and the boundless sky.

The sense of tranquillity and at the same time of the richness of every moment never again possessed the Nameless One as fully as it had during the few years of his life on Green Bowl. Next to the woman whose name was Elil.

He had always entered into greater contact with the beings of other worlds and had delved more deeply into their lives than had his comrades. The other members of the expedition devoted themselves to problems of power sources and mathematical analysis of fields of force. They exchanged information with scientists and engineers: the language of figures was truly universal. But the Nameless One studied differences in the biospheres, ethnography, and forms of intellectual development. On lifeless planets, he conducted excavations.

In the course of their long journey, he was gradually losing the sense of being only a son of Laola-Lyal. The complex shape, the oneness of the entire universe, revealed itself to him: from eras of steaming oceans on fiery beds of magma he would go on to silent dead worlds of porous pumice. Life spread before him in its most astonishing manifestations: from colloidal-oxygen structures to crystalline formations yet unrevealed to any eye, and—guessed rather than seen—in the guise of spheres of energy, of formless condensations of forces.

Yet all of this—in only one-half of infinity! The second half—the mysterious antiworlds—were still concealed. Leaping across the abyss of time, creating its own time, conquering space, would the reasoning mind ever attain absolute knowledge?

In appearance, Elil was very unlike Likhé. They were as different as their planets. It was not at once that the Nameless One had learned to see the beauty of Elil.

She was the daughter of several stellar races. After the cosmic catastrophe, which had attracted the attention of other inhabitants of the Equinoctial Galaxy, the decimated mankind of Green Bowl willingly mated with newcomers. New currents poured into the veins of the subduers of the waters. Their appearance changed, their capacity to grasp the new expanded. Their culture developed and became enriched.

The Nameless One was drawn to Elil by the special music of her lineaments and features; she moved and spoke as others sing. In her, imagination predominated over rational analysis. She and her people lived in fantasy as freely as the Laolitans did among facts and figures. This captivated and disarmed him. For the first time imagination, dream— the mocked and exiled child of reason—had found a home. The Nameless One, who had once so carefully concealed all tender impulses from the keen and merciless eyes of Likhé, was appalled, next to Elil, at his own poverty of feeling. It was as though half of the beckoning world of Green Bowl remained hidden from him. He could distinguish contours, sounds . . . then everything would melt away.

On warm starry nights, which were not black like the depths of space but alive and glowing—with the reflected constellations inhabiting the waters like strange fish—Elil talked to him about Green Bowl. In his own galaxy, Laola-Lyal was the only inhabited planet. And therefore for a long time the Laolitans believed that intelligent life was the greatest miracle, granted to them alone. Instinctively, they thought of the universe as a hostile place.

Elil was, on the contrary, full of good will. Her eyes regarded everything around with attentive gentleness. She did not consider reason a privilege reserved solely for manlike creatures.

"Why do you assume," she would ask, "that the world is made up of unconscious atoms and that your thought is the center and the starting point of everything? Before we came to the idea of the screw, there were already spiral flower seeds prepared for distant journeys. Or think of underwater plants— how selflessly, heroically, they tear themselves away from their birthplace in order to fecundate the open flower cups awaiting them on the surface?"

"Such 'wisdom' belongs to the species as a whole," argued the Nameless One with some annoyance. "It is only by chance that nature attains its goal: it conquers by multitude."

"Of course," Elil agreed. "But the possessors of a brain are not the rivals or the masters of nature— they are its collaborators."

Yes, that was something she lacked utterly—the instinct to dominate. She was all giving, all goodness, without a trace of harshness. A whole chain of generations had nursed along their ailing planet and gradually revived it. Respect for all manifestations of life became the inner law of every individual.

The Nameless One felt with shame that, in coming infinitely far in their knowledge of the world, in measuring it out in weights and numbers, in rejecting all power of the miraculous over their minds, the inhabitants of Laola-Lyal, that wise old planet of the violet zone, had at the same time impoverished themselves and neglected their own vineyard.

"Close thine eyes and put out thy reason," Elil read aloud an ancient incantation. "I speak only to that which is below reason. To the nighttime self that rules the body. Creation is the work of the imagination, not the will."

He listened to her voice as one might listen to ancient runes that had been buried in the depths of consciousness and now were rising, rising to the surface. . . . And already he was recognizing them, acknowledging them as his own. . . .

A thousand years ago—Elil told him—the world of Green Bowl had been torn by wars and hatreds. One day some visitors from outer space had landed on the planet, but the means of travel and communication were still imperfect at that time. The visitors had not been able to rise again or even send news of themselves back to their own home. They remained on Green Bowl forever. Their descendants, armed with great knowledge, put it to evil ends. They became the founders of a ruling race.

The era of repression lasted many centuries. People were born and reared in fear and servility. The high technology brought nothing but suffering.

Anger and protests broke through from time to time, and one of the rebellions was successful. A part of the planet abolished oppression. But the world in which there were no slaves had to defend itself against the forces of the slave world. Green Bowl, which at that time was mostly dry land, with massive mountain ranges, was like an island in space, whose inhabitants were at one another's throats. An endangered island, for scientists discovered that a stray bolide was moving toward the solar system of Green Bowl out of the depths of cosmic space.

For a long time the scientists could not determine the nature of the bolide. A terrifying hypothesis arose that the cosmic body consisted of antimatter. The threat of extinction hung over everything. Life became unbearable. Frightened humanity sought refuge in old superstitions. The world that had long discarded its gods and devils was now repopulated by dark forces which threatened it invisibly on every side.

Wild tales that mingled fact and fancy succeeded one another. It was during those troubled decades that a new, sensational rumor swept Green Bowl—about another race, a third one, which inhabited the mountainous regions of the planet. This race, it was said, had never had any contact with the civilized world and was still living at the level of the stone age. There was general excitement. Everybody wanted to see the mysterious "ice man."

The new sensation diverted people's minds from the impending danger. And expeditions were dispatched to the highest mountains by the two hostile camps, impelled as much by rivalry as by scientific interest. The expeditions met in the region of eternal snow, upon the only road leading to the heights. After some days of violent clashes, they made a truce and went on fairly peacefully, for both groups were quite small, and the life of a mountain climber is harsh and demands mutual help.

However, at every camp site arguments on social, moral, and racial problems flared up between them. Out of the arguments, some common truths began to emerge, gradually wearing down the fanaticism of both sides.

As they continued their upward journey, they began to come upon visible traces of the "ice men"— footprints, remnants of their meals, entrails of birds and rodents, which no animal leaves behind. The possibility of encountering the "ice men" increased.

When the first shaggy figure was seen dashing past a cliff, a new dispute broke out. Should they try to capture the "ice man" alive, or shoot him down? Yet what if he was truly not an animal but an intelligent being?

The two expeditions had to decide on a common plan of action and hence a common moral code. It was a moment when the old enmity could either fade away in mutual agreement or sharpen to the point of violence. . . . But all their conflicts were reduced to insignificance by an event more frightful than anything that might have been foreseen.

In the morning they awakened to find the sky beneath them (they were very high now) aflame with silent, terrifying light. Many centuries later an ancient epic was to describe the catastrophe in these words: "Dense pitch poured from the sky. The face of the earth turned dark, and black rain fell. It poured down day and night. . . ."

The panic-stricken people rushed down. But soon their instruments recorded a dangerous thinning of the atmosphere. The unexpected seemed to have occurred. Instead of settling when the bolide invaded the atmospheric belt, the air rushed upward from the ground. The little that remained was only in the region of the highest mountains. For how long? The people could do nothing but hope that, after the bolide had passed, the violent upheaval would subside.

Ascending again, they feverishly began to search for refuge. Wonders of courage were performed in the attempt to find a way around the icy summit. But even there their instruments warned of danger. They huddled together, a pathetic little band. Some, unable to endure the tension, shot themselves. Some lost their footing and plunged into the abyss. All were demoralized. Around them wandered groups of "ice men," but nobody was interested in them any longer.

A fierce snowstorm broke out and surely would have buried even this small remnant of mankind had not one of the "ice women," moved by a glimmering of pity and perhaps by a maternal instinct, dragged them like so many puppies into her own cave. And there they lay, sick and dazed, until the warmth of the fire and the animal skins beneath them returned them to consciousness.

And it was then, in the smoke of the ancient beneficent fire, that they first found within themselves the strength and courage to look at the disaster face to face. The world had perished. Their miserable world, torn for so long by senseless strife. Their splendid world, with its bountiful land, its greenery, its singing birds. All civilization, all science. All their women and children. . . .

Aside from them and the tribe of "ice men," it seemed that nothing living had survived. They lay by the fire, thinking painfully. There were no conflicts, no arguments now. The old errors became glaringly obvious to all, and rightness no longer needed confirmation. The disaster convinced everyone beyond a shadow of doubt. Mankind had failed to unite in time to deal with the danger. From then on, life would have to be lived differently.

It was then, too, that the first dim outlines of the

future order and future ethics began to gather, like early glints of light, out of the utter darkness of despair.

The survivors evolved four principles, four voluntarily adopted laws. The first law banned suicide as the gravest crime against the future. The second proposed that every man try to recall and write down everything he ever knew, beginning with the multiplication table. The third was a decision to join the tribe of the "ice men" and bring up their future offspring in such a way that they could span the whole historic gap dividing their parents and carry on the culture of their fathers. And lastly they were to lay the foundation of a society based on justice and equality from its earliest steps. They took a solemn oath to do all this. And they fulfilled it.

The Founders were still alive when galactic neighbors landed on Green Bowl. Detecting signs of a catastrophe, their stellar ship decided to go out of its way and descend on the stricken planet. This happy chance, which brought them active aid, saved the remnants of the planet's inhabitants, or their belated insight might have been no more than the last testament of a doomed race. A species has its own statistical laws: small numbers do not survive. It was only the arrival of the ship that helped the tribe of "ice men" to become the forebears of that intelligent humanity which the cosmonauts from Laola-Lyal found on Green Bowl.

The Nameless One wondered whether the harmonious world of Green Bowl might not be the prototype of the future of all rational societies. The young, almost primordial race of "ice men" had skipped long stages of painful growth; its fresh response to the world around it was combined with an advanced culture and a social order that precluded force. Technical thought had had no time or opportunity to destroy vivid emotions and imagination. The two currents merged, with neither suppressing the other—a brotherhood of myths and numbers.

On Laola-Lyal, mentographs had long been used to correct not only speech but also thought; they provided the most precise, most economical means of expression. But with Elil, words rose and were suffused with living light in response to the moment. The word gave birth to the concept and became emotion. It was often far richer in meaning than thought itself.

The Nameless One spent a great deal of time with Elil. On the eve of his group's departure for the uninhabited satellites of Green Bowl, he had broken a leg, and it was necessary to graft in electrodes in place of the torn nerves. He was left behind to convalesce.

Several leading technicians of Green Bowl went with the Laolitans; it was there, on one of the barren asteroids, that a place had to be found for the future center for the manufacture of the energy-producing substance.

In the beginning, when the Nameless One was quite alone and had to lie on his back without moving, he probably would have felt lonely and depressed in the alien world, were it not for Elil.

Those long days between sea and sky remained engraved in his memory forever: the slight rocking of the large raft on which he lived; the streaming, bright reflections on the canvas walls. Around him there was so much light and sun that he literally drank them in with every pore. The artificial radiation which sustained the cosmonauts inside their space ship could never gladden and caress the body as living warmth did.

When Elil had first come to him, the Nameless One thought she was a doctor or a nurse in the floating hospital where he had found himself. She would approach him and take his hand and touch his forehead with her fingers. He assumed that this was treatment by hypnosis, and he willingly submitted to it.

They had long medical conversations. He learned that on Green Bowl the genetic programs of the future inhabitants were not subjected to any changes; the evolutionary process was not interfered with. The only thing permitted was slight corrective action. How could man satisfy his immemorial longing for immortality? Being was seen as indivisible. The

present, the future, and the past existed simultane-
ously. The rational creature was programmed in such
a way that he could see only his own sector of the
road. His psychological time was limited. However,
time as such did not exist at all, according to the
thought of Green Bowl; it was merely the structure of
space itself. And each person felt himself a link in the
immense chain of life.

The Nameless One listened and compared. On
Laola-Lyal everything was mathematically predetermined: a child simply could not be born different
from the rest. But on Green Bowl there had evolved
a special regard for the individual: the chain must
not be broken! The inhabitants of the planet re-
spected themselves as the repository of the past and
as the bearers of the future.

To the Laolitans, progress meant the attainment
of the absolute ideal—ideal health, intelligence, and
beauty. They had reached instead a universal same-
ness. On Green Bowl, however, perfection was seen
as the wealth and diversity of individual features, as
the ability to feel the extraordinary—and to transmit
it to coming generations. Its society was predicated
on inner independence and originality of thought.
The planet's inhabitants were not against machines,
but they were against everything that demeans and
limits man in a machine civilization.

The Nameless One felt a brief pang of resentment.
Elil's words struck at his own planet, his own era.
The Laolitans might be dry-hearted, but it was to this

dryness that he had given his youth. And yet . . . and yet, he thought, the fires of youth are never wasted. The future is crystallized of many things on many levels.

He learned that Elil was conducting experiments with the second intelligent race on the planet—sea animals who possessed the rudiments of speech and thought. As for her concern with the Nameless One, it was due to . . . .

He stopped listening to her words. She suddenly became significant in herself, as though separating out of the generality of Green Bowl inhabitants, whom he had seen for such a long time as a facelesss mass.

The difference in her appearance ceased to disturb the Nameless One. He knew: though strangely set, Elil's eyes, soft and warm as the eyes of an intelligent animal, were turned to him not only with curiosity but with tenderness. Their light remained with him long after she would go.

He learned to recognize the plash of her boat, no matter how far she docked it: a quivering line of biocurrents stretched between them. But this was not an ordinary contact! Or was it that he already wished it not to be ordinary?

He wondered more and more about what still remained unknown to him in her. What would she say or do? What echo would be wakened in her being if he should kiss her, even once?

But it was not yet love. It was a search that, like a

cluster of light rays, probes deep in various directions. Love came in time and, blindly, cruelly, was not recognized until too late.

Hurtling through space, the Nameless One looked before him with unseeing eyes. Red and lilac sparks glimmered dimly on the screen. Velocity blurred all colors. Stars were almost invisible. Worlds, worlds. . . .

Thank you, Elil, for having been, with your warm smile and tender eyes, which wept at parting.

Thank you, Elil, preserved now only in my dreams, but in reality long fleshless, melted like an icicle under the ruthless rays of Time. . . .

MOMENT OF ETERNITY

"I bless the ceaseless pain
That leads the way—
I'll burn in its flame.
The acrid taste of salt,
The bitterness of earthly grass
I bless."

ODAM, naturally, did not believe Lilith's story about the monsters of Salt Lake. Nevertheless, he went there on the following day.

He returned thoughtful and confused. The rabbit carcass, gnawed by ants, the woven basket with the honeycombs, and the dry lumps of salt were there. No one had touched them. But there were tracks on the shore. . . .

He could always tell unerringly the reason for every broken stem, every tassel of grass seed scattered by the chance blow of a hoof. He could easily determine the size and the weight of an animal from a single footprint. But he could neither explain nor understand the meaning of those hollows, that scattered sand, the furrows in the scorched grass. An odor unlike the odor of warm-blooded animals still hung faintly in the air.

Lilith waited for Odam with impatience. But he would not speak. Silently he handed her the things she had left behind; even the salt had lost its value in his eyes.

He walked to the river and sat down on a rock. The air and the water were veiled in flowing silver mist, as in the emanation of some mysterious breath. In the rifts, the nearby shrubs were dimly green. Each breath was followed by another, spun of the same mist. Here and there a sun ray pierced the veil, glinting, wavering on the surface of the water.

Around him lay the familiar, unthreatening world. But to Odam it had lost its old solidity. Some strangeness entered their lives that day. Neither of them knew the word "love," although it had been love that led them from the tribe. But now it began to lessen, to subside, like a river after floodtime. Their longings and desires diverged, were much too different.

Odam instinctively feared any changes: they brought anxiety. The greatest safety lay in the known, the customary. Having left the tribe, having committed a stupendous, revolutionary act, he tried, as it were, to forget it as completely as he could and live as much as possible as he had lived before. In the beginning, he had even become more rigid in his ways than he had been before.

Odam remained the slave of old taboos, but Lilith was forever striving after freedom. From birth, she had possessed a special gift: no matter how low she tried to bow her head, even her immobility betrayed her. The impulse toward the marvelous, which for a time had slumbered in her soul, awakened irresistibly within her.

Day after day she patiently and keenly sought out the tracks of the mysterious beings. She circled and circled around Salt Lake, like the gray eagles that nested in the cliffs above it.

Lilith was gulping air with an open mouth. It took enormous effort not to flee. She had seen the monsters several times, but always from a distance, pressing herself down in the grass, hiding between rocks. But now she had been seen. She was sure of that.

The sight before her eyes transcended all of her experience. Her dark mind worked quickly, linking up chains of analogies, tying up different objects with connecting threads. She was motionless. Yet even as she waited, she was in dizzying flight—she was approaching the unknown.

But the unknown was also approaching her. It made one step, then another. The round eye, which took up half the head, turned in her direction. Then she saw that the eye was transparent, and behind it were peculiar features with other, smaller eyes. They were strangely set and shaped, but they resembled man's eyes.

The difference in the stranger's appearance from that of her clansmen did not especially disturb Lilith. At the dawn of civilization man occupied so modest a place in the world that he did not regard himself of singular value. Every day brought confrontations with the new. Animals and plants, one stranger than the next, passed before his eyes as fully equal denizens of earth.

Why, then, should Lilith worry because the Nameless One's eyes were covered with sliding membranes that met in the middle instead of lids with a fringe of lashes? What did she care if his forehead was wide and bony, his head large, and his body squat?

Later she was equally unshaken by the story that stars were inhabited. The mind of a savage is capable of leaping effortlessly over any abyss. When the simple and the complex are not differentiated in awareness, nothing can be especially startling.

The Nameless One and Lilith were approaching each other cautiously, but without particular anxiety. He knew a great deal about the inhabitants of the universe. She knew nothing. And this brought them together. They looked at each other with eyes full of curiosity.

Lilith smiled faintly. The strangers laughed readily and often; she had seen it from her ambushes. But this was the first time that she felt their eyes upon her. There was something in the stranger's eyes that drew and hypnotized her. Still uncertain whether this was a sign of danger or of friendliness, she tried to free herself. Her lips closed with intense effort.

And immediately the Nameless One's eyes released her. As if breaking out of an invisible snare, she straightened up.

"Strangers! Where are you going?" she asked loudly, trying to control the involuntary quivering of her fingers. "This is not your hunting ground. The mountains and the woods don't want you!"

Lilith's voice seemed pure and ringing to the Nameless One. He knew that sound is only the vibration of air waves at a given frequency. Yet he had never heard such sounds before. He looked around him in confusion; there was nothing nearby but field flowers. Not the kind that thickly cover forest clearings, greedily and hurriedly entwining their stems, thrusting their roots into the darkness. No. There are flowers that grow singly, in the open. You can see them from a distance. The wind does not sweep over them carelessly; it plays delicately with each separate cup. If that large bluebell had a tongue, it probably would speak in Lilith's voice. Her voice did not float, did not envelop. It shaped every syllable with the purest clarity. That was how it struck the Laolitan when he first heard her.

He had to decipher the speech code of the Earthmen. This was not easy on the spur of the moment, without special instruments. Language had been the first organizing force on Laola-Lyal as well. But the alphabet method of thinking had long been abandoned on his planet. Speech seemed an obstacle, it slowed communication, and new forms were evolved, transcending words. The Nameless One knew that the language of the Earth woman he met was primitive, but he did not possess the key to it. And yet he had to answer somehow, if only to reassure her, to win her trust.

And he pronounced in funny, guttural tones the first combination of words he had caught: "Strangers, where. . . ."

At first, Lilith looked intently at his mouth. Then, with a sigh, uncomprehending, she bent her head to her shoulder. The guttural, rumbling sounds were repeated.

"Strangers where," the Laolitan enunciated more carefully.

She finally recognized the distorted words of the Tabunda language. How funny those monsters turned out to be! They could not speak! Lilith narrowed her eyes and gave one of the most intelligent beings in the universe a glance of condescending tolerance.

And for a long time, from her point of view, the Laolitans remained far from perfection: they did not know the simplest things. For, indeed, they did not understand the language of Tabunda; it was very difficult for them to learn it. And Lilith never suspected that there were tongues other than hers.

The Laolitans had long since dispensed with figures, too. Their machines did all the calculations for them. Their knowledge of fire was only theoretical, and one day one of them put his hand into the fire. Lilith laughed at his silliness, but then she wrapped his hand in a soft leaf, cool and moist, and the pain ceased. The Laolitan looked at the healed skin with almost childish curiosity.

How could the daughter of Tabunda know that the distant Laola-Lyal was already at the end of the photon era, compared to which even the nuclear period would seem like the stone age? In their pride, the Laolitans were now criticizing travel along light rays as mere slavish adherence to the curve of space.

"What about movement by explosion?" their scientists would cry impatiently. "What about rebellion against the known and the search for new forms?" "The photon current helps the ship; it would be irrational to reject it," protested experienced sky pilots. "But are we to follow forever the stream of photons which obediently circles gravitational fields?" the others argued. "Why not attempt to master the flow of directed time as well?" And so a new abyss to be explored was opening before the Laolitans: the two-sided abyss of macro- and micro-worlds!

But Lilith could not know anything of this. Her contact with the Laolitans was slight and superficial. And yet she not only absorbed from them but also taught them. Long accustomed to the obedient power of mechanisms, they were astonished for the first time by the agility and omnipotence of bare human hands. The primeval joy of muscular exertion enchanted them. They, who could instantly strike any target at any distance with the directed ray, now threw stones at trees or flying birds. And they were so incredibly clumsy that they laughed at their own failures.

Her sense of superiority—if only in the smallest things—freed Lilith of all fear. She played an honest game with the Laolitans: it was an even exchange. She felt herself their equal, and that is always the first step on the road to trust.

Lilith vaguely sensed that the Nameless One's

speech was somehow different from hers and Odam's, even though they now used the same words. The Nameless One continually added complexities to the language: he combined the names of objects in new, unusual ways. Lilith's smooth forehead would wrinkle with the effort to understand.

Her wariness melted away from one day to the next. And as her trust increased, she found it ever easier and more exciting to listen to the Nameless One. On the other hand, she felt with growing chagrin how much more difficult it was becoming for Odam to follow what she herself was saying.

When she first brought the Nameless One to the cave, Odam turned gray with pallor.

"They do not look like us," he whispered. "Did they come from the other side of the world?"

Lilith burst into laughter. But Odam's face was constantly becoming gloomier. They still lived side by side and sometimes caressed each other. But they were rapidly diverging, like two streams coming from the same source but already divided by a mountain chain.

The Nameless One toiled like a wine-maker, opening empty bottles and filling them. Such was his work over Lilith's mind. He filled it with ideas. Then he would turn into a weaver: he bound the ideas with threads—closer, tighter. . . . He joined and criss-crossed the threads, creating a web. And then he boldly cut it, shaped it into images, thoughts, assumptions. He was creating a whole universe of thought.

It was as though the Nameless One were standing at the very cradle of intelligence. But he himself no longer was merely a well-intentioned observer. Changes were ripening within him, too. The moral arrogance of the Laolitans grew more and more repellent to him.

The Nameless One's eyes, glinting with yellow and green, studied attentively the life on Earth. His eyes saw "faster" than Lilith's. What seemed like a single solid ray to her was seen by him as a complex interplay of twinkling flashes. In order to see continuous, unbroken light, he needed a frequency of flashes a hundred times greater than that required by her eyes —as though every unit of time contained more instants for him. But he remembered that on Green Bowl he could not see beneath the surface of the water, while Elil had possessed both "upper" and "lower" vision. One was adapted to the atmosphere, the other to water, where she saw clearly things that to him were no more than dim shadows.

Here, on Earth, he could distinguish in twilight the finest nuances of color, while Lilith seemed to be blinded—everything before her merged into grayness. The sun dazzled him in the morning not only with the stream of rays perceived by Lilith but also with its piercing ultraviolet rays. An alien sun with alien rays!

How many of them he had seen in his wanderings!

He merely had to close his eyes for picture after picture to pass before them. The greenish-white glimmer of condensed gases falling upon jagged cliffs, unworn by rain or atmospheric flow. Galactic spirals that seemed so near, one might have thought they were the chief source of the planet's light, and below —vast, glasslike deserts with translucent spheres: a world of crystalline formations. The white flame of a star intolerably hot when you approached it, yet remote and offering no warmth to the eerie planet it illumined.

Or else a dark sun, with a crimson rim that made the sky a livid violet; and over the planet, the yellow, transparent stream of gas, trailing behind the ascending light-plane—a cold, wild, useless world!

On other planets the light-plane had to surround itself with a protective shield of currents. Forked lightnings wandered over the surface of the shield as over an invisible sphere. Sometimes they merged into continuous streams, rivers of powerful discharges, and these deadly rainbows, beckoning, deceptively blue, flowed and flowed, silently flashing and fading beyond the ship's armored surface.

In the hermetic helmets there were also shields; they had become obligatory equipment for cosmonauts after several Laolitans who had carelessly turned toward glowing bodies had lost their sight. After that, even withdrawing from some alien azure sun, they were cautious in observing both its corona, with its shifting lilac patterns, and the rays reflected like water dust in the ghostly wake of the speeding light-plane.

In the depths of the hottest, gleaming yellow star they saw violet clusters, darkly lit from both sides. Bubbles of gas burst and flew up—enormous as planets, yet seeming weightless to the eye.

When the giant intergalactic ship of Laola-Lyal had reached its destination, deep in the Milky Way, the count of galactic spirals became the guideline to its location: some light-planes left it along the level of the fifth spiral; others went down the vertical of the third.

The Nameless One's group had to explore the space around three stars. The Sun was the last of these.

The light-plane had circled for a while around Jupiter without landing; the radiation belt around it was a hundred trillion times stronger than that around the Earth. Nor were they drawn to the enormous rocks that made up the ring around Saturn—a greenish-yellow and grayish-lilac icy planet speeding along a stretched ellipsis. They spent some time upon the plains of Venus, coated with a crust of hardened volcanic glass. They watched the pseudo suns flaming over Mars: its atmosphere, saturated with icy crystals, strangely, almost menacingly, refracted light.

Into all their calculations, the Laolitans introduced

the "coefficient of ignorance"—consideration of the forces still unknown. And Earth, with its teeming life and dense atmosphere in the midst of a cosmic desert, presented itself to them as a "coefficient of miracle." Its discovery was a moment of triumph.

The Nameless One never ceased wondering at the tenacity of earthly life. As it originated on Earth, he thought, life must have had to grope for ways of development: there were no models, no analogies as yet, for trees or fish or humans.

Studying his surroundings, the Nameless One supposed that the early terrestrial creatures lived within a limited range. But some seemed to have tried to "break through" space: dolphins dived into the depths and rose into space; monkeys ran up and down trees, from root to crown, and to them the world acquired an added dimension. Later living beings attempted to "shift" space itself. Instead of approaching food, they tried to bring it closer to them—to pluck the fruit and bring it to their mouths.

But when had man himself originated? When he picked up a stone and broke a nutshell with it? Or later, when he first scratched out the crooked lines of ornaments? Or still later, when he dimly felt a fear of death or pity for living creatures or had, perhaps some early intimation of self-awareness, of growing knowledge of himself?

And, then, was the terrestrial intelligent creature the crown of a long process of evolution? Or merely the happy mutation of an ancient ape, which had once battled with a mountain lion and fled to safety in a cave with a high radiation level—a relic of the primordial era of stormy changes on Earth? Did an accidental genetic leap occur under the impact of this radiation?

The Nameless One had too little time for exploration and study. Earth was to remain to him a book he was allowed to read but briefly. Yet it absorbed him from the very first page—he read and read, and whole continents of flame arose before his eyes. . . . But the book would have no ending for him. He would retain mere fragmentary glimpses and surmises. He would turn the pages in his mind, puzzling about the unread parts. Whence, from what darkness, Lilith, have you come to your Earth. . . .

"Don't you see, don't you feel?" Lilith asked him once, as she inhaled with pleasure.

"I have forgotten how," the Nameless One answered guiltily. "I have been flying in space so long. And now, with you, I am recalling everything again."

They stood under the dark-red branches of a tree that gave off the balsamic odor of early autumn. The odor was as sharp and expressive as the touch of a hand. The Nameless One looked pensively at Lilith. To her, all objects seemed to possess a radiance, while he saw light but felt no joy in it. The son of an aged planet, he could not feel the rapture of the child

—of the first denizen of paradise—that filled her, an Earth woman, at contact with everything alive.

The Laolitan took deep breaths, forgetting that he had not been born for this rich, fragrant atmosphere. Were it not for the protective devices, his lungs would have been burned by the dense, fiery oxygen. He kept his eyes half-closed—there was too much light on Earth. Even the rays of the spectrum seemed to be refracted here more freshly and vividly.

And next to him stood Lilith. They were divided by millennia, by the abyss of civilizations. But she knew nothing of it. He alone knew.

She stood barefoot on her young planet, and her eyes—gray, long—looked keenly at her surroundings. Her world was simple. In the distance, over the russet hills, blue clouds floated like smoke.

"Ah, you winged creature!" whispered the Nameless One.

He seemed to have forgotten that she was a savage. Enchanted, happy, he relished his involuntary humbleness before her.

The way of two beings toward each other is not simple. It is almost as long and full of curves and turns as the way of heavenly bodies flying in the emptiness of space.

The Laolitan did something Lilith did not understand. He brought his face close to hers: his lips were pressed to hers! For a fraction of a second, a thought flashed through her mind: he meant to bite her. Otherwise, why bring his mouth to hers, although, as she had noticed, it was not filled with teeth but firm small lamina that easily could pinch the skin.

Her impulse was to leap back and defend herself. Her hands were stronger than his—she knew that! If only he didn't put to use some magical object he had slyly hidden from her until now.

But he was not trying to cause her pain at all. He remained in the same strange, unnatural position, motionless. And if she had not felt the violent beating of his heart, she would have thought he had fallen asleep.

Indeed, he looked asleep. His eyes were shut. It seemed to her that his head would momentarily drop off his shoulders. Lilith supported it—she put her hand behind it. This was her first movement. A muted sound, like a moan, broke from him. But at once he threw back his head and she saw a transformed face. Everything was strange at that moment. A warm wave swept over her heart.

"You're not afraid of me?" he whispered.

"I'm not afraid of anyone," said Lilith, trembling lightly.

He said something in his own tongue. She did not understand. And in her tongue there was probably no word like it. He repeated it over and over, and he looked as humble as a man who had not taken part in the hunt and now stood by the fire, vainly hoping that somebody would throw him a leftover piece.

In her tribe there was a stern law: those who don't hunt receive no share. And yet once Lilith had slipped a piece of smoky meat on a bone to such an outcast. But then his eyes, which had resembled those of a cornered animal, changed suddenly: he snatched the bone from her and ran triumphantly to the side. He did not give Lilith another glance; gratitude was unknown to the people of Tabunda.

But the Laolitan's face remained kind and trusting. He continued to look at her expectantly.

Then suddenly he clutched at his chest. His face darkened, his cheeks turned hollow. He jerked oddly, suffocating, yet at the same time pressing his hand over his nose and mouth, as though he were trying to stop his own breath. As she looked, he leaned sideways, like grass drying up in overpowering heat. It was like the work of an evil spell. Lilith did not know that he had merely exhausted the dose of enzyme that allowed the Laolitans to breathe the Earth's air without a helmet.

The boundary between living and dying is always terrifying to man. The knowledge that a moving, warm being similar to oneself is turning into something cold and motionless before one's eyes is intolerable at any level of development.

At first Lilith was merely frightened, then she was stung by pity. With a cry, she lifted the Nameless One. His eyes rolled back, his lips were black as coal.

She ran in long bounds, carrying him on her back as a female animal carries her injured cub.

The big egg was not far. Lilith pushed the Nameless One inside, clambered in, and slammed down the lid.

But the egg remained motionless and did not hum from inside, transmitting its vibrations to her whole body, as it did every time she stepped into it after the Nameless One. However, the lid shut tightly and turned several times by itself. At once, a light went on—dim, grayish—and something began to happen to the air. The Laolitan's breathing became more even, the blackness began to disappear from his skin. But his eyes were still half open, without sense or recognition. Lilith, on the contrary, felt an acrid dryness in her throat. She breathed more and more rapidly, like a fish thrown out on the sand. Yellow and violet circles swam before her eyes.

Like every savage, she dreaded illness. "If I go away now to the other side of the world," she thought, "there will be nobody to save him."

And she strained, not her memory, which was excellent—whatever she saw once remained imprinted in her mind forever—but her will. With a trembling hand, Lilith touched the control panel. She did not know what she was doing, but she repeated the Nameless One's movements in their exact order as she remembered them.

The egg shook, the trembling communicated itself

to her body. There was a steady hum, and they rose into the air. Lilith turned the handle until the wavering arrow on the white disk reached the precise position in which it had been recently, when the Nameless One was taking her to the "whole hand," as she still called the five Laolitans to herself.

The egg flew fast, but Lilith was already scraping her cheeks with her nails. Something was pressing her from within—she gasped for air. The gray light, which grew brighter in the cabin, was turning dark before her eyes.

Only her will and her incredible animal memory prevented her from making a mistake: she brought the egg to the light-plane.

The Laolitans—there were two of them near the ship at the moment—saw the flying capsule tumbling, bumping drunkenly as on invisible ruts, and immediately switched on the automatic distance controls. Obeying their will, the egg evened out and landed without mishap. Unscrewing the lid, the Laolitans dragged out the two unconscious forms. They left Lilith on the grass, but hurriedly carried the Nameless One into the ship. He was, indeed, suffering acute poisoning from terrestrial air.

If Lilith had delayed bringing him to the flying egg with the atmosphere of his own planet, he would have been dead. Lilith, on the contrary, was almost suffocated with the lack of oxygen in the cabin, which also would have killed her if she had stayed in it much longer.

The Laolitans, however, did not know for a long time what had happened. They thought that the Nameless One had flown the egg himself; in the beginning they attributed his story to delirium. How could the apparatus have risen, they thought, and followed the correct course if he had lost consciousness while still on the ground?

When they wanted to question Lilith, she was already gone. She had recovered her breath and wandered away. With a heavy head, exhausted from the nervous strain, with a vague sense of bitterness in her heart. Where was she going? She did not know. The egg had carried her to another part of the world.

"You abandoned her, helpless, on the grass?" cried the Nameless One as soon as he came to.

They looked at him without comprehension.

"Your life or death was a question of minutes. We could not be distracted."

They were unquestionably just and well-intentioned. Even self-sacrificing when their work demanded it and certainly fearless and loyal to the very end. But they were completely devoid of compassion. The Nameless One felt a chill invade his heart as he looked from one clear, stern face to the other.

They tiptoed away, trying to make no noise and exchanging glances. He was still so weak. They could not understand why he had found it necessary to push the native woman into the flying apparatus, how he had managed to reach the ship in that state of shock, and why he denied that he had been at the controls.

The sun was much too hot. Lilith rose from the grass. On one side loomed the white bulk of the light-plane, gleaming intolerably in the vertical rays of the sun. On the opposite side, the forest looked temptingly green and cool.

She wandered off across the scorching midday savannah, and the leaden sun pressed down upon her head. Her body was covered with sticky sweat, and her nostrils seemed unable to draw in a single breath of air. Her half-collapsed lungs strained with enormous effort.

Herds of strange animals—hump-backed, with twisted horns, or spotted and with incredibly long necks and tiny heads—ran in the distance, seeking refuge in the thickets.

Lilith stumbled upon an animal watering trail and, forgetting caution, followed it, driven by a thirst more violent than fear. She scarcely noticed when she entered the deep green twilight of the forest, dotted with the brightest of unknown flowers. Clusters of buds cascaded down like golden rain from slender, twisted stems. The scarlet cups of orchids flamed in the warm, humid air. It seemed that in this forest the butterflies and birds and flowers recognized no other colors than golden, emerald, and fiery red.

The river had spilled over here into a quiet, reed-grown lagoon, and the heat-weary foliage streamed in it in silvery, moist reflection. Water fowl, dazzling white in the sun, like lumps of snow, stared motionless at the bottom. Tiny fish and water insects fearlessly dashed back and forth between their coral feet. A gray heron with fluffy, lowered wings stood in the shelter of a berry bush; the berries glowed vividly, but the satiated heron barely touched them with his beak. Once in a while he turned an incurious eye to the reflection, where a similar bush, hung with berries, streamed in the water, glittering in the sun.

Lilith bent down to the water and drank and drank like an exhausted animal, feeling no taste, but merely gulping to soothe her parched, dry lips and throat. Unable to tear herself away, she went deeper and deeper into the water, until her tattered grass skirt blew out like a sail and, torn off by the current, floated down the stream.

Suddenly she felt as though something had struck the back of her neck: the mysterious power of human eyes compelled her to turn. She still sensed this invisible stare; it was palpable as something she might be holding in the palm of her hand. And all at once a scream of terror broke from her lips.

Not more than a dozen steps away, a black-spotted animal was drinking greedily. It may have followed her down to the water, or else she had not noticed it before. Its body arched sinuously, the feline head turned, snorting—and just as Lilith screamed, the beast sprang to its feet. Its legs were long, straight, powerful, and pliant. The animal gathered itself to leap, but then another body, like black lightning, burst from the thickets. There was a whine as of a flying dart, and the animal vanished behind the wall of greenery.

All this took less time than it takes a falling stone to strike the earth. The red-eyed fish still darted in the shallow water, and the lazy herons barely moved their beaks.

Stunned, Lilith looked around in confusion. This forest was entirely unlike anything she had ever known. Hadn't she just seen before her a slender beast covered with thick fur, with black spots forming broken stripes along its back? Hadn't a black-skinned man stood a few steps away from her, holding a curved twig, its ends drawn together with a string? It was a weapon unknown to the Tabunda. The man had a wide face with high cheekbones, a round chin, and a protruding lower lip. On his broad chest rested a narrow stone shaped like a crescent moon, with one polished horn. His overhanging brow lent his face an air of sternness and at the same time generosity.

All this was mysterious, extraordinary: there was no trace now either of the man or of the beast!

Driven by the instinct of self-preservation, Lilith rushed to look for a way out of the imprisoning forest

—back to the plain, under the shadow of the infrequent trees, to the grasses singing in the wind like
tightly drawn oxgut.

Her way was barred by the gnarled tendrils of
lianas, giant ferns with hard, waxen leaves, mushrooms, lichen, orchids, trees—not a spot of ground
bare of the tangled greedy network of greenery.

Sometimes she leaned her ear against the earth
and heard a distant thunder as of an earthquake: a
herd of elephants was coming, and she had to turn
aside not to be crushed by the gray giants. But her
ear also caught the chopping sound of the hooves of
herds of buffalo; the savannah was somewhere near.

Lilith stopped many times, exhausted. When at
last she made her way out of the thickets, the light,
the air, the earth were yellow. The sun, not yet completely gone, was setting behind a solitary tree,
spreading around its flat, layered branches an aureole
of glowing dust. Clouds floated slowly toward the
horizon, absorbing the glow, wavering, turning fiery
red. Streaks of gray blue, edged with intolerable glitter, would obscure the sun, and then the earth became still yellower. But gradually the glitter cooled,
and a dense evening cloud rose like a guardian in the
west, with a jagged edge that flashed for the last
time like a polished stone.

Herds of herbivorous animals hurried to find a
safe refuge for the night. Their shadows flitted
among the shrubs; the clicking of hooves was heard

on all sides like the chattering of grasshoppers. The savannah was subsiding into silence, preparing for sleep and defense.

Lilith climbed the solitary tree and sat without stirring among its branches. She was as quiet as she could be, save for the beating of her heart. For in the open any movement betrays you! And night life was awakening all round. Snorting, mewing, menacing roars, the padding of soft paws surrounded her with danger on all sides.

Suddenly the darkness of the savannah was pierced by a narrow bluish ray. Like a giant tentacle it wandered over grass and trees, and the beasts scattered in panic before it. Then, from somewhere in the sky, came a booming sound in which the voice of the Nameless One could barely be recognized.

"Lilith! Where are you? I am looking for you. Come toward the light, Lilith!"

The voice circled over the savannah like a bird that has lost its fledgling, now approaching, now receding, and the gleaming blue ray swept through the air, tearing the darkness.

But Lilith sat without stirring, her eyes tightly shut. Like the animals, she was terrified of light after nightfall.

The Nameless One found her at dawn. Standing under the tree, altogether naked, she stared as one bewitched at the gourd filled with water and the bundle of fruit in a soft skin.

"Lilith! At last!" the Nameless One cried out joyously, stretching his arms to her.

She turned, but immediately her glance went back to the mysterious food set out for her by some unknown hand.

He saw that her lips were slightly parted with tension and her eyebrows met like two rivulets flowing in sinuous streams. She seemed to listen to something in the distance.

"What is the matter?" The Nameless One asked anxiously.

She smiled absently, impatiently. She was as incapable of speech now as the forest itself, though it is never at rest, because the wind constantly ruffles its branches and flying clouds blow cold and moisture at it.

Lilith was silent as the grass is silent, although it rises as the earth breathes, although it grows, stirs, furls, and unfurls, And what can be more voiceless than the water that streams and disappears between your fingers? Yet where do the most violent storms arise? And what is the human heart but a small sliver of the elements?

The Nameless One understood nothing of this. He took Lilith by the hand and led her to the light-plane. She did not resist, but she kept glancing over her shoulder at the tree with the straight gray trunk. The first rays made its bark seem pink. The sun had risen over the savannah, and everything that lived in it was happy. Lilith walked with a secret smile. . . .

Colors and sounds! A whole world which Lilith had seen without seeing, heard without hearing. Until now she was excited only by smells—richly sweet or acrid. But what had she known about color? About pale blue, which did not disappear in mist? About violet, which had so quickly put her to sleep on that single night she had spent aboard the light-plane, after the Nameless One had found her in the forest? About the soft pale yellow of the robes worn by the Laolitans inside their plane? About dismal gray— the color of twilight, the time of forest killings, of ambushed quarry?

In sounds, Lilith usually noticed only their vibrations, the raising or the lowering of tone, the growing force of a blow. She never thought of their meaning, unless it was a direct signal that concerned her.

And now she stood motionless, struck by an unknown stream of sound, petrified, with pupils dilated, everything within her shrinking. A weight seemed to press down on her chest; it crushed her and at the same time seemed to open all her veins; invisible blood flowed out of her body.

The music sprayed her with bird song, trilled and whistled, swelled, thundered, and laughed. Power and delicate melody followed one another. The earth became less and less material under Lilith's feet. The pain of ecstasy filled her. The color drained from her cheeks and lips, and finally, with a faint sigh, she softly sank into the grass.

The melody went on for a few moments longer, then the Nameless One switched off the stereophone. The first music lesson was finished.

On that morning when he had found her in the savannah and brought her to the light-plane, Lilith quickly mastered the use of sleeves and clasps. Within a minute she appeared in the silvery overall of a cosmonaut—and suddenly there was no savage! Instead, there was a slender youth, his long gray eyes throwing a sidelong glance around him, intelligent and slightly shy.

A miracle had taken place before the eyes of the skeptical Laolitans: involuntarily they began to see Lilith as an equal.

Although they were engaged in a great task, the Nameless One's companions remained as they had been: their thinking was confined to the standards of Laola-Lyal. It was only the Nameless One who had developed a longing for cosmic fellowship. Now he often thought as a poet. This seemed strange and archaic at a time when Laola-Lyal was entering an age of nonverbal communication. And yet it was precisely the thinking in images that brought him to the threshold of understanding new and different modes of existence.

His association with Lilith had revived the verbal instinct in him: he was overwhelmed with the desire to pour himself into a liberating stream of words. (How vainly the patient Elil had waited for this!)

"Listen to me," the Nameless One would say, lightly touching Lilith's forehead. "Listen, and let nothing astonish you. I know that all of this will enter your mind as in a dream. But let it remain there even as a dream.

"The silence of thought, the long silence of flight . . . you will not understand this, Lilith. You do not know the structure of the universe, the structure of the brain. You think your hand moves by itself. . . .

"There was an ancient idea that thought is the fastest thing in the world. Well, then, what if thought should really fly through space at a speed of its own? Faster than anything else? What if it really became the first messenger from the world of supergalactic velocities? If only you could, for a single moment, conceive of this vast range of possibilities! Movement of bodies in space would then be almost unnecessary, archaic. Only thought would travel! It would give signals, establish contacts, exchange information. Thought would be caught by telescope, as light is caught today. Amplified a millionfold, it could be sent out as a greeting to every galaxy. But, then, perhaps what seems fantastic to me now has long been a reality? Just think! Perhaps it has always existed on the other side of the universe, in the mysterious world of antimatter? What if the people of the anti-world have never known any other means of communication? Lilith, Lilith, I am only an ordinary creature with a brain, from an old galaxy of the violet zone. But sometimes I feel that, truly, my thought is immortal and all-powerful!"

He seized her hand. His green eyes opened wide with excitement and instantly closed again: the light struck his pupils as sharply as a whip. His eyes closed, he felt a tremor run over Lilith's skin—the unconscious muscular reaction of a primitive being frightened at an alien touch. But she did not snatch away her hand. She conquered within herself the ancient instinct of separateness. And when he opened his eyes a little they met her look, painfully struggling to cross millennia.

And a sudden thought—strange, vague—flashed, not through his mind, but through his heart. A thought that pierced the Nameless One with kindness and compassion: shouldn't his journey in Time come at last to an end? Did not his duty to Laola-Lyal recede now before his duty to the wild young Earth? What more could Laola-Lyal gain from him, one of the million cogs of its excellently functioning machine? His almost infinitesimal drop of information? But it was so easily replaceable. Could he ever convince the passionless, all-knowing Laolitans by the mere power of his words that their ideal civilization was deficient, warped? Life itself would teach them in good time—through the great confrontation of cultures and ideas in the universe. He would not live to see that day. His own lifetime was limited, and on Earth he would burn out even faster. Yet he would have enough time to do something for the Earthmen. He would explain to them the simplest principles of mechanics, show them how to make some tools. Whatever he could do here, his life would not be wasted, just as the lives of those who climbed the cliffs of Green Bowl were not wasted. Their daughter was Elil. His would be Lilith.

It was only now that he realized how much he loved her, how deeply he was filled with the eternal longing to give her all of himself.

"But what a responsibility! I will be answerable to your future for every action, even every thought," the Nameless One whispered, looking with anguish at the russet hills brushed with the green of grass, whose colors he saw somewhat differently from Lilith. "To feel within myself the chain of many ages, the link with many lives. From now on nothing will die within me; the thread will stretch out forward—but where?"

"But I don't want it!" said Lilith suddenly.

He often forgot that she was listening to him with fierce greed even as he thought aloud, and that something of his words managed to reach her mind.

"I want to be free," repeated Lilith. "To go wherever I wish, without thinking about anything. I do not want to fear life as you do because of some chain! I shall stand in the forest and shout to all the beasts: bare, bare your fangs at me, growl with your red maws. I am stronger and more cunning than you anyway. I shall climb the mountain and be taller than any tree!"

"Why, Lilith?" the Nameless One asked in confusion. Her savage cry had broken into the measured flow of his thoughts like a sharp spearhead. "Why?"

"Because I want it so," she answered stubbornly, throwing her arms wide open.

He gave her a sidelong glance. Strange! No matter how many worlds he had visited, his time of learning never ended.

The sun was low, and the western rim of the ocean boiled coldly. In the east was spread a blue-black plain with white-capped waves that looked like coastal dunes. The rollers thundered with ceaseless menace. A leaden line divided the water from the misty sky.

Dark shadows gathered in the hollow footprints— the heavy, almost square ones of the Laolitans, and the narrow, flying ones of Lilith. Her feet left on the smooth sand a patterned imprint of the grasses of which she wove her sandals now.

But her steps slowed down as she approached the water and the familiar savannah was left behind. She was afraid of the sea. It had its own voice, and its breath was so powerful that it shut out all the other smells. Lilith walked with her mouth open. She was breathless with the salty wind; it terrified her and intoxicated her at the same time. Suddenly a nimble wave ran, hissing, at her feet, and scalded them with freshness. Lilith sprang back.

But only a moment later she was beating the water with her palms. She fingered the foam like strands of hair, and laughed, turning to the Laolitans her narrow face with its gray eyes which now looked blue.

The Nameless One called to her to come back, because she went in deeper and deeper and the foam covered her shoulders.

Envy and sorrow stung his heart: they, visitors from space, could never enter the Earth's waters naked; they were condemned to live within the prisons of their suits, equipped with gravitational lining and devices to warm or cool them as the outside temperature changed. He tried to recall the sensation of the living wind of Laola-Lyal, but his skin refused to reproduce the memory—it existed only in his mind.

All of his life and his long journey from Laola-Lyal, he reflected, occupied no more than the briefest moment of eternity.

For a long time he sat in silence. The print of Lilith's bare foot still remained in the sand.

But if the part of the universe we know, he asked himself, is only the stellar universe, what place is allotted in it to the individual? Why does the rare, infrequent spark of life flare up on distant, unconnected islands? What does it bring into the world? Matter is prodigal; in order to create the smallest thing it spends immense amounts of energy. However numerous the stars, however overwhelming their mass may seem, they are pouring out their existence in streams of photons. There is an eternal, ceaseless shifting of stellar substance in the universe.

And what of thought? Could it have been born of the instinct of self-preservation? Can it be that matter seeks to protect itself by thought? And that the creatures possessing brains are but a form of the struggle of organized matter against entropy? Unquestionably the mind will be perfected more and more. Is it impossible to put an end to the dispersion of the stellar substance? The useless loss of thermal energy in space? Today it is impossible. But we shall find the means to do this, too. We shall eventually create an army in defense of stars—a truly celestial army!

"Come back!" the Nameless One broke out of his meditation.

Lilith's head had disappeared under the water. A mound of white foam rose in place of her shining eyes and black hair, scattered by the motion of the water like the arms of a medusa.

Drawn by this shout, the Laolitans threw an indifferent momentary glance at the stormy ocean and the courageous bather. They were absorbed in silent but animated discussion about the admixtures in the white sand of the dunes and the concentration of salts.

The Laolitans were in a hurry. The time allotted

to them on Earth was coming to an end. Their most precise quantum clock indicated the point of return, and the arrow was moving implacably toward that point. In the depths of the Milky Way, in the system of the double star which was a part of the galactic nucleus, they were awaited by the intergalactic ship on which they had left Laola-Lyal a thousand years ago. All the investigating light-planes that had been wandering for the past three centuries among the planetary systems had to return now with their information.

What would they find and what would they discover on gathering together once again? Who would be missing?

The Nameless One stood helplessly at the water's edge. Lilith was being carried away farther and farther. Over the roar of the ocean waves she had not heard his call. Death—absurd, unnecessary—hung over her, and all the might of Laola-Lyal was powerless to help her!

And suddenly—as Lilith had in the jungle—he saw a black body darting from the height of a dune. Was it a man? The proportions of his body were astonishing in their harmony, like those of a flying bird. For a moment he disappeared in the white seething foam of a breaker, then he dived out of the next wave, far away. The frenzied ocean flew after him; its surface was alive with gleaming, moving, sunny flames.

Dimly, as through blue crystal, the Nameless One

saw two bodies, like two fish, gliding and soaring in the water, flying up over it, dipping again into the sun and salt, vanishing. This lasted endlessly. A thousand times they perished and revived before him. Until the tide threw out the two upon the shore and sped back, leaving a line of hissing, crazy foam on the wet sand.

The man recovered a second earlier than Lilith. He raised himself on his knees and looked into her face. He seized her strongly with both arms, and at that moment her eyelids quivered: she recognized him.

When one face is pressed to another, four eyes merge into one, and this mysterious eye with a diamond spark of white looks deeply, darkly. . . .

The Nameless One rubbed Lilith's cold hands. He spoke to her rescuer in Laolitan, repeating something ardently again and again. Both of them finally turned their eyes upon him. The Nameless One switched on his automatic translating device: the man answered. His voice poured freely and strongly from his chest.

His short curly hair lay in a close line just above the horizontal fold on his brow—a fold intelligent and unexpected on a clear, young forehead. He bent down to pick up from the sand a robe of fine skin—a handsome robe, soft and beautifully wrought, which he tied at his throat with a string made of tendons.

"What did he say?" asked Lilith avidly.

"His name is Emerald. He lives in this country. He asks if you have come down from the Moon."

"May his dreams come true and his desires be fulfilled," said Lilith hurriedly, pressing her hands to her breast. "No, not from the Moon."

The sharp sound of the signal spread over the dunes: the Laolitans had finished their work and were returning to their flying capsules. Emerald anxiously raised his head, looking for the singing arrow in the sky. But Lilith did not even turn.

"I am Lilith, a daughter of Tabunda. Tell him."

"We must go, Lilith," the Nameless One said, tugging at her sleeve. "Remember, your home country is far."

The signal was impatiently repeated, and Lilith's slender neck, unconstrained by amulets, bent low. Her nostrils quivered as she wept. Turning for the last time, she looked with sad eyes, as though from a deep gorge, at the man lit by the slanting rays of the setting sun.

Emerald stood motionless upon the dune.

"Return!" his voice called to her, already from afar.

Yes, the Nameless One no longer felt himself to be an atom of Laola-Lyal. He had acquired his own, individual being; he held the entire universe within him. What was he to do with it?

The decision to remain on Earth demanded courage. He knew it, and would have been glad to borrow some of it from the Earthmen.

There are, of course, different conceptions of courage. To Odam and Emerald it had a very definite meaning: to be courageous was to act in spite of fear.

The men of Laola-Lyal had long lost such simplicity of thought: problems were not decided by a single blow of the fist. The Nameless One understood the relativity of visible actions. He knew that it was possible to move forward with dizzying speed without making a single motion. Odam was a stranger to all duality; to him, running meant running. When the muscles are at rest, the mind can fall asleep, too. Such was the natural order of things—as natural as the succession of day and night.

But Lilith? The Nameless One passionately longed to leap across millennia. He watched the savage, mysterious, enchanting life of her spirit with both chagrin and tenderness. At times he was ready to laugh at his own obstinacy, for he was far from young. It ought to be time for him, as for a wise, gnarled tree existing in the world of silence, to give lessons in patient indifference. But unexpected sounds are sometimes born in the heart of the wood—resonant, young, fresh —and he listened to himself with wonder. It seemed to him that every step he had taken in the universe until now was but the gathering of scattered parts of a single riddle. In the harmonious world of Green Bowl, among the whirling rocks of the ring of Saturn, everywhere he had compared and studied what he saw. The vector of courage was defined with sufficient clarity: it meant rushing forward without certainty of return. The parts of the riddle had been collected one by one. To grasp its meaning—that was the thing that demanded courage, ten times more of it than all the earlier efforts and sacrifices. For the field of his duty, he felt, had grown incomparably wider than what he now saw as the narrow sense of duty of the Laolitans.

On the eve of departure, he told them of his decision to remain. They seemed prepared for this.

"Impossible!" all four replied.

"Who can forbid me? I am a free Laolitan."

"Certainly," they said. "But only on your own planet. Outside its sphere you are helpless. The breathing enzyme is not stable, and we can leave you a very small reserve. In order to renew it, you will need a whole laboratory equipped with photon energy. You are a part of Laola-Lyal. You cannot exist outside it—none of us can."

The Nameless One was stubbornly silent.

"You know it yourself," they went on. "How long will you be able to last here after we leave? You will suffocate. The excess of oxygen will burn you up."

"And yet, before that happens, I shall be able to do at least a little to help Earth."

"The dim mind of men cannot absorb much. Your efforts will be wasted, don't you see it? And Lilith? She will be still unhappier to lose you in such a dreadful way, knowing that she had been the cause of it."

"She may not guess it."

"She knows it already. We told her."

The Nameless One threw back his head; his eyes flashed anger. He wanted to cry out that no one had the right to limit his freedom or make a choice for him. But the words died within him. It seemed hopeless. His distant planet held its inhabitants with bonds that were perhaps even stronger than those of the primitive tribe of Tabunda; they existed within the very being of every Laolitan, not outside him.

"We all belong to the Great Task," repeated the cosmonauts. "Who can free us of it? You have invented for yourself a fantasy of the equality of all galaxies," they went on patiently, "and based it all on the mere fact that the chromosome system of the woman of Green Bowl had turned out to be compatible with ours. The birth of a child is a frail foundation for a philosophy! The mind of Laola-Lyal has long outgrown the age of arbitrary conclusions."

"But if we are so omniscient," the Nameless One persisted, "why do we retain in all our calculations the 'coefficient of ignorance,' allowing for forces not yet known to us?"

"In order to prevent technical errors. All structures in nature are the traces of former motion. Mastery requires the knowledge of origins. And observation is the process that links space and time. The mechanism of the universe is complex."

"And the mechanism of the soul?" cried the Nameless One.

They did not answer. They were no longer speaking the same language. Yet the Nameless One tried again.

"The chain of associations may differ with the observer," he spoke wearily. His anger had subsided to sorrow. "Don't you admit the possibility that other intelligent beings might draw other, perhaps more profound conclusions from the same facts?"

"We have not met such beings," the Laolitans answered haughtily.

"Yet what criteria can you apply in judging one mode of functioning superior to another?"

The Laolitans shook their heads.

"We have Laola-Lyal. For its sake we are ready to sacrifice all—but only for its sake! Our journey into space has been a matter of necessity, not choice."

"But no!" the Nameless One cried out. "The concept of a 'homeland' will inevitably change. The diffusion of civilizations must spread to the very boundaries of intelligent life. There can be no question of superiority or domination. Our only question should be: what will be our place in the world? Our marvelous civilization has enclosed itself within its own self, it is in danger of degenerating into something monstrous! The subordination of everything to utility and fixed norms has banished growth, courage, the element of risk. No, if Laola-Lyal wants to remain alive, it must learn to think differently. And it is not my chance realization of this truth that will compel it to do so, but its own venture into the universe."

"Well, we must leave that to Laola-Lyal itself," his fellow cosmonauts replied. "Our light-plane is expected at the orbital cosmodrome. For the moment, our chief problem is to break through the force belts once we leave Earth, so as to eliminate the velocity differential at docking time. We are leaving in three days."

"I must go, Lilith," said the Nameless One. "I shall never see you again, and you will not see me. It is a thousand years since we left our own earth, and it will take another thousand years to return to it. Laola-Lyal will welcome those who have survived. Its people are enduring and disciplined; everybody is equally healthy, strong, intelligent, handsome. . . . No, but you will not understand any of this, my poor Lilith . . . my happy Lilith, for mankind still faces a million years of searching. If only you could know how much I love you and your Earth!"

He spoke the word "love" not in the language of Tabunda, where it had only a narrow and primitive meaning, and not even in his own language, once used by the ever-smiling Likhé, but in the language of Elil, in which the word was deep and rich and glowed from within.

"Yes, I love you," he repeated as simply and freely as a man breathes. "And I am infinitely grateful to you. You have taught me that my heart is not dead. And this is a discovery as great as the discovery of a new star."

"Never see you again? What do you mean?" Lilith's eyes opened wide. "Won't I come with you?"

The Nameless One shook his head.

"Don't you remember how you could not breathe inside the flying capsule? And that is the only kind of air we have."

"You mean, I will remain alone? We shall never again come down near the Big Water? You will not show me the plains of White Snow? You will not tell me about the sky? Your light-plane will go up and up, and take you farther and farther away? Forever?"

"Yes. We shall fly through black space. The flight will be neither long nor short, but infinite. I will have taken my turn at the controls no more than two or three times, and you, my Lilith, will already be dead. There won't even be anyone for me to dream about. Endless generations will live out their spans on Earth before we reach our planet. And we shall still live and live, fly and fly. . . ."

Lilith's face trembled. With a wild cry, she fell upon the ground. Her hair spread on the grass as though a tree had scattered all its leaves at once.

The Nameless One looked at her sadly. How violently youth grieves! Loss and misfortune seem unbearable to it. But only the mature man knows true despair. Unrelieved by tears, it weighs one down like a gravestone. A future without hope. . . .

"No!" Lilith cried suddenly, raising her head. "I will not remain here! If you do not wish to take me with you, take me to Emerald's country, to the edge of the green wood where you found me that morning, when a gourd filled with water stood under the tree. I want to see the spotted beasts again. Emerald will teach me to send a flying dart from a bent twig. I shall not be frightened of the salt sea again! I shall learn to live under the sun that melts everything inside you."

"Yes," the Nameless One agreed gently. "It will be as you wish. Go say good-bye to Odam."

Lilith turned away her face.

"I do not sleep in the cave anymore," she whispered. "Odam lights his own fire."

The Nameless One felt shamed and humbled. Busy with his own thoughts, he had ignored too much in Lilith's life. He knew how shaken Odam had been at their coming. Unafraid of the strongest beast, Odam retreated before the unknown: he had tried to placate them, even to bring them sacrificial offerings. The Laolitans had never been able to reach him. Superstitions, almost a religion, were being born under their very eyes, and they were helpless to do anything about it.

Gradually Odam had transferred some of his timid bafflement to Lilith as well. She had begun to frighten him. He never touched her anymore.

"Well, then," the Nameless One said shortly, with a farewell glance at the hills, the distant mountains, the yellowing trees. It was the month of the gathering of acorns. "Come, I want to show you a few more things before I leave. We don't have much time."

He spent all that day explaining to her the use of the lever and building the simplest implements for her. He taught her an easier way of making fire than that used by the people of Tabunda. Bending a twig, he tied its ends with a synthetic string and looped the string once around a pointed stick. Then, setting the stick vertically in the small hollow carved in a piece of wood, he showed Lilith how to move the bow to make the stick revolve. This way, it took less time and effort to get fire. Some days earlier, he had taught Lilith to attach sides and a keel to a raft, thus making it more stable in the water.

At the appointed hour, the light-plane rose and circled for the last time above the Earth. For a brief moment the plane halted over the African savannah, where it borders on the ocean.

Like a tiny silver spider on a glittering thread, Lilith fearlessly slid down from the height and for the last time raised her hand in greeting—a gesture she had learned from the Laolitans. At once, as though out of nowhere, Emerald appeared beside her —an agile, muscular being who still continued to measure courage by a skillful leap.

They crossed the sun-bright clearing. A moment, and they disappeared among the tree trunks. Lilith. . . .

The membrane slipped over the Laolitan's eyes.

Later the Nameless One watched on the viewing screen the misty outline resembling a filled bowl, and in it—a shiny heart-shaped drop, like a cat's eye in the dark. But the huge hand of the cosmonaut on duty passed across the screen, blotting out the view. And when it cleared again, the drop was gone, lost among millions of others.

The ship of the Laolitans soared into the familiar regions of curved space. Lilith and Emerald remained on the flat Earth. For thousands of years this would be how men would think of it: flat, motionless, without breath.

Yet one human had already seen the blue sheath of the atmosphere around the Earth. Deep within her, she carried the indestructible germ of human questing. Lilith—the primal mother of the future! The children of her children would long to spread the boundaries of the universe. And we know better than anyone else whether they have succeeded.

ODAM SAPIENS

"... And, like a child, he started
Probing and weighing nature."

THE TRIBE of the Tabunda lived for a long time in the bountiful foothills, till one night thunder struck in the northeast. Its rumbling grew louder and louder, and the horizon began to glow with a strange, livid light. Thousands of birds broke from their nests, darting about in the air with wild, sharp cries. The wind, which first rolled softly over the grass, began to hum, bringing the smell of fire.

The tribe abandoned camp and rushed under the trees for shelter. The steppe fire quickly reached the very edge of the forest. For a whole week, an eerie brownish light just barely seeped down from the sky through the thick pall of smoke. Twisters of flame swept over the plain, and a steady crackling and snapping came from somewhere in the dusty murk. Sand, smoke, and burning grass flew through the air. The wind was now so violent that the flying grass burned out before it could set fire to the treetops. Only the trunks were marked with traces of the fire: their bark was charred like burnt skin.

For days the people of Tabunda fled south, away from the fire, but in the end it caught up with them. Roaring, it scorched their hair and clothing, and swept on. What had been a flowering valley became a desolate plain covered with fantastic patterns of ash.

The women wandered over the still warm ash, gathering baked lizards, mice, and birds. Children feasted on fried roots. But the men were gloomy. The rich hunting ground was gone. It was necessary to search for a new place.

Before long, devastating torrents of rain came bursting down upon the uncooled earth. Layers of earth and stone slipped from the mountains; streams tumbled down, carrying clay and rocks.

The tribe climbed up the mountains to escape the flood. Breathless, terrified, the people reached at last a plateau of hard rock, resistant to destruction. Little by little, the horizon began to clear. The sun lost its frightening brown tinge. Prisms of feldspar glittered serenely with blue sparks. The polished surface of the rocks flashed red with bits of garnet. But none of this was noticed by the people. They were hungry, exhausted. The children were sick. At the boundary line between sand and ice, nothing grew but spotted lichen that formed varicolored patterns.

The tribe began to descend, crossing mountain canyons where winds were always howling. Its path lay close to the Salt Lake. And there, the young girl Heva, who had not yet gone through the initiation rites, found Odam's footprints.

She told no one about her discovery. The two who had disappeared were never mentioned anymore. The people thought that Odam and Lilith had long crossed over to the other side of the world. But to young Heva he was still alive. Her thoughts were constantly returning to his image; she saw no one to equal him among the young men of the tribe.

Heva had round cheeks, filled with the sap of the sun. A sweet honey smell came from her, as from the skin of a ripe fruit. She differed little from the other girls of the tribe. She was simple and a little cunning. Not simple enough to tell her thoughts; cunning enough to keep to herself what she did not want others to know.

Nobody noticed any change in her, and yet from day to day she went farther away from the tribe, lost herself among the rocks, seeking out signs visible only to her. A broken twig, a bit of flattened grass, a lost dart tip spoke to her about the direction where she was to search for Odam. Heva would return to camp after hours of absence, hiding her bruised feet. One day she did not return altogether. They looked for her in the vicinity, but in the morning they had to go on.

And so, separating from the tribe, Heva came down one day from a mountain meadow overgrown with tall, sparse grass to the bottom of a canyon, into a gray-brown wood. The ground there was soft with rotting leaves. The trees were too dense. From lack of light, their trunks were covered with some pallid, unhealthy growth.

The lower branches, dead, devoid of foliage, stretched darkly above her like arms of skeletons, and the crowns, rising high above, shut out the narrow bits of sky. The wood was cold and damp, and only the invisible birds high in the treetops sang out with voices of hope.

Heva's round face, with eyes that seemed only to mirror the surrounding world, had grown thinner. Her usually merry lips were tightly shut. She walked without stopping, subsisting on raw roots and grubs she found by digging in the earth around decaying stumps; they buzzed with a muffled sound like dry rain.

When she heard the distant roaring of some beast, Heva superstitiously touched the three wolf teeth strung on a tendon, which she had worn around her neck since childhood. Her neck was strong and shorter than Lilith's. The hair over her forehead was curled with perspiration. And it was thus, perspiring, and breathing heavily as after running for a long time, that she appeared one day before the astonished Odam.

"I see you," she uttered the customary greeting of the Tabunda, boldly, yet modestly.

Her short skirt made of grass fibers indicated that she had not yet emerged from adolescence, although she had tied it below her waistline to seem older. The skin was delicately gold on her bared belly.

"I am Heva, a woman of your tribe, and I have brought twigs for your fire."

He was silent, and she spoke again.

"The tribe has gone on farther. I flattened the grass and left a tuft of hair. They think I was devoured by a panther. I do not ask you about Lilith, whom you have led away from the tribe. A man does what he wishes. I came to stay with you, if you permit me. If not, I will go and catch up with the people of Tabunda. I ask for one thing only: give me some meat for the road and a dart to defend myself against the beasts."

She fell silent and stood with meekly lowered eyelids, to allow him to examine her without hindrance.

Gradually he began to remember: she was the first child in the tribe to be born with yellow hair. Everybody considered it a marvel. Now her hair was long, and she had tied it with a grass string. It covered her back, but left the breast and shoulders bare.

Though younger, Heva was taller and stronger than Lilith. She had capable hands, which now hung submissively along her sides, and strong feet, now ankle deep in field daisies and wild dill, which had a heady fragrance after the recent rain.

Heva's full lips smiled faintly, and when she raised her eyes, Odam saw that they were not gray and long, like Lilith's, but round, like a deer's, and blue.

"Do you command me to go?" Heva asked plaintively.

"You can stay," Odam said, looking away. Something contracted in his throat. He suddenly realized that the past was gone without return. The demons, who had put a new, rebellious heart into Lilith, would never give her back to him.

But now he would not be lonely either. Before him stood the short-legged Heva, a daughter of his own tribe, obedient to his laws in everything.

And curtly, with a quick nod, as is proper for a man, he ordered her to follow him into his cave.

When he had first remained alone, Odam felt nothing but relief. His mind, unsettled with too many incomprehensible events, could rest now.

The Laolitans had disappeared, and with them the metallic odor they left on everything they touched. Young grass had hidden the hollows left by the huge gray eggs that were gone forever. Life had returned to its normal course: the day was inevitably followed by the darkness of the night.

Odam whittled his darts and diligently carved on them the broken lines—symbols of successful hunt. But his lines did not resemble the splendid, powerful beasts with red horns which came from under Lilith's fingers. Odam lived in silence. Silently he hunted, built fires, chopped trees with his stone ax.

He went farther and farther in search of quarry. A man who lives by hunting must cover wide ground. Besides, no one waited for Odam in the cave, making him wish to return as soon as possible. He could even stay away as often as he wished.

At one time he developed a craving for the intoxicating juice of henbane. But oftenest of all Odam sat still with a fishing line, looking at the water and dreaming. His dreams were of the past, not of the future. The river was not wide, and it reflected entire trees, from bank to bank. In the midday stillness, life went its own way in the water: circles spread over the surface from the waterbugs; tiny spiders skimmed along, guarding their allotted patches. The sun, made silvery by the clouds, sent down a bright spot over Odam's birchbark float. The spot expanded, glittered, and the float disappeared, perhaps because of the sun, perhaps because a fish had pulled it down. Waking from his reverie, Odam tugged at the line. Heva was calling him from the distance in her singsong voice, so unlike Lilith's pure, clear sounds, which he would hear no more.

Heva's arrival changed little in Odam's life. Of course, he saw that she was a good home-keeper, persevering in her tasks, devoted to him. Nowadays dry maple and hazelnut twigs were always lying ready in the morning by the hearth; they burned evenly, without sparks. In the evenings, Heva drove off the clouds of gnats and midges with smoking pine roots. She made skillful use of her strong teeth—an additional tool with which she cracked bones, bit off small twigs. The stars neither frightened nor fascinated her, as they had fascinated Lilith. When a familiar constellation appeared in the sky, she knew that it was time to go out in search of ant grubs.

Heva was a diligent wife. But what in Lilith had been beauty and directness was turned in Heva into cunning and seduction. Odam saw this. How much he had learned to see!

The very air was in a whirl around Heva. She moved quickly and made instant decisions. From the very first, she sensed the presence of Lilith's threatening shadow and launched a struggle against it.

It seemed to her that Lilith was wandering nearby; she did not understand that it was possible simply to leave. Though in the past she had sometimes been obliged to walk great distances together with the tribe, she never noticed these distances. She had always been enveloped in her small world, as a seed in its shell, and this world moved with her. If Lilith was alive, then she would surely return to the only inhabited world! And Heva had to watch for her appearance day and night. To catch the moments when she would burst in with a gust of wind or sit down by the fire to dry her hair.

Heva unerringly guessed even the most fleeting presence of her rival. She guessed it from Odam's empty gaze, his suddenly lax movements. But a woman should not rob a man of strength; she should give him strength! If she is a true woman!

Heva carefully examined the wood and clay utensils in the cave: crude bowls and trays, birchbark baskets and wooden drinking cups. They were decorated with colored carvings. The pale hues of the clay were intermingled with the bright juice of berries. Every piece of wood or rock that could in some way be useful in the household bore traces of sharp "drawing stones"—a whole pile of treasures carelessly abandoned to a stranger's hands!

Heva fought the impulse to throw them into the fire. But her native shrewdness told her that things, like men, lived longer in memory once they were gone. She pored over the patterns and colors with the eyes of a watchful lynx. And gradually hatred sharpened her vision and the instinct of rivalry entered her fingers.

One day Odam found Heva absorbed in mixing colored clays with fat. He was astonished. So Lilith's magic was possessed by another woman as well?

Distrustfully he sat down near her. Heva did not raise her eyes as she painted designs on a jug. She had progressed in her secret learning, for she no longer repeated the same drawings. Her own designs emerged under her fingers. They were simpler and seemed to cling more closely to the jug.

"I know what juice must be pressed to get this color," Odam said, touching one of the old vessels.

"You will show me," said Heva without turning from her work. "But look: isn't this color brighter?" And a fresh line of carmine red appeared on the stone palette.

"It is," Odam admitted, rewarding her for everything with those two words.

And suddenly Heva made an unconscious movement: in concentration, she passed her little finger lightly over her upper lip, as though outlining it. It was Lilith's gesture, Lilith's alone! Odam felt as though it had been stolen from the dead.

But Odam was mistaken. Heva had simply brushed a drop of perspiration off her lip.

Losing interest in the painting, Odam rose on weakened legs, and Heva sensed again the presence of the shadow. . . .

Time went on and on—time, which people did not yet know how to count or measure.

One day something blue-black, like hot soot, flashed behind the bushes. Odam started violently. For a moment it seemed to him that he was seeing Lilith's hair. He did not even wonder what he would do now that he had Heva and their children. His heart throbbed like a young man's. Earth and sky regained their old colors. Everything changed suddenly.

He stood without stirring, as if still waiting. But yellow-haired Heva slipped to his side. She ran a suspicious glance over the silent, motionless bushes.

"What did you see there?" she screamed in a shrill voice.

"I thought . . . I thought I saw black hair," Odam muttered, as though waking up. And instantly he knew that he should not have said it.

Heva's face twisted into a crying grimace, but her eyes glittered drily. She rushed toward the bushes and struck out at them. The rounded body of the peacock she had tamed burst out from among their stems. The tail spread open like a starry sky. The regal bird was scrambling away at top speed.

Heva stood with her arms akimbo and roared with angry laughter. There was no Lilith there, nor her accursed black hair that magically bound other women's husbands and then tantalized them all their lives. She was not there and never would be!

Odam walked away, stooping. Heva did not call him. Now that she remained alone, her excitement vanished. She felt unhappy and drained. So she had to be afraid even to this day of the return of that barren creature!

She was filled with bitterness. But she compressed her lips and went back to her daily work—preparing food and rearing children. What could the wife of a Tabunda hunter think about? Her lot was patience.

And Odam walked away into the young, still sparsely growing wood that had risen on the burned-out ground. The wood was filled with sunlight. Clean dry grass lay underfoot, and the straight, slender shadows of the tree trunks slanted across it. Odam expended as much effort in stepping over this illusory fence as though he were climbing up a mountain, although the ground was level.

A strange emotion took possession of him. He seemed to have forgotten all the years with Heva, and Heva herself, who was no more than a few hundred steps away. But he had a clear and vivid memory of

Lilith. Especially of how he had won her, how he had taken her despite the whole tribe, how they had left, intoxicated with youthful courage, and lived together among the rocky foothills, in the cave he had long since abandoned. They had felt as though they were the first humans on earth. There was no one to teach them. It seemed to Odam now that he had been as bold and resolute as Lilith, that he had risen with her in the large gray eggs of the Laolitans—and there was no fear in his eyes.

Oh, yes! That had been a time when he had breathed deeply and time passed quickly. And now he was condemned to live without living, and die without dying. . . .

Yet, in time, his sharp longing for Lilith which drove him he knew not where, which made it impossible for him to settle down to any task, tormenting him until he did not know what to do, how to escape it, subsided into a gentler sorrow, a kind of inner warmth. Odam had reached the age when even the strongest feeling can no longer rule all of a man's energies. He came into the period of creation. The desire to work became all-absorbing. He became more even-tempered and kinder to Heva. The distant wandering light no longer burned him but clarified his being from within, gradually illumining his mind. He, too, wanted to know! And not only to know but to embody his knowledge in tangible form.

In pensive concentration, he would turn a piece of wood or stone in his hands hour after hour, recalling what Lilith had told him about the instruments of the Laolitans. And his growing sons would squat around him on their haunches, following his every movement with Heva's round eyes. Four of them had dark hair.

The graying Odam looked lighter than his eldest son. The youth's hair was as shiny and black as coal, but in the sun it sparkled like a snowy mountain summit.

There was something in this boy resembling a young, high-strung dog. His nostrils sniffed for a lost trail. His eyes, gray and deep-set, like a young owl's, looked sharply forward. It would not take much time before they reflected a transformed world. One day they gleamed with tears of ecstasy: his father was talking about the heavenly flying eggs.

"In the middle," Odam said, "there was a heavy box, and that was where the power of movement came from. It flowed into two large tubes like elephant trunks at opposite sides. There were two rows of openings in them, above and below. The forces they sent out struck the earth, and the jolts gave motion to the eggs."

His sons listened with open mouths, ready at any moment to rush off in search of these mysteries. Wonder will never die out in the world! And no matter how careful Heva may be, her children will be enticed away from her by Lilith. And so it will be ever.

Oftentimes, Odam would lead his little band for a

whole day to places far from home. It might be to a
shallow stream, to slip a hollowed log into the water
and fasten sides to it with wooden pegs—the frail
beginning of shipbuilding! Or else it might be high
into the mountains, where the bottomless sky glittered, vivid blue, and shadows were bright upon the
jagged cliffs. And always he found occupation for
every hand. He never felt lonely anymore—he had
his work to do.

A day came when Odam, Heva, and their half-
grown sons returned to the tribe. They had much to
teach the people of Tabunda. The only thing of
Lilith's he had brought to them were the designs of
blue clay on his sling, though now they were made by
Heva. With teeth clenched, she would rub and scrape
a yellow bone or a white stone and cover them with
pictures—and many others learned her skill. But
does it matter who had been the first? Only the aging
Odam still remembered. In the evenings, he took to
gazing at the stars. In silence he watched them rise
and move across the sky. And, dozing off, he heard
his own voice of that distant time when flowers
bloomed more brightly and the waters plashed with a
clearer, ringing sound: "Why are you standing there
so quietly, Lilith?" "I try to understand the voice of
the night." "What do you want with the night? We
have a hearth with glowing coals, we have just eaten
meat and roasted fruit. What do you see, Lilith?"
"I see the breathing of the rolling mist, its white hair

trailing on the grass. The day is tired, it is going to sleep. But what is happening out there, beyond the mist, when night comes? I shall go and spread it with my hands. . . ."